A SURG

Sister Alix Rutherford had been offered
the job she wanted more than anything
else in the world—running an operating
theatre at the Central London Hospital.
It was a dream come true, until
suddenly she was faced with an impossible choice . . .

Elizabeth Harrison started producing magazines at the age of ten and, she says, 'excruciating novels, usually unfinished (just as well) from about thirteen.' She was equally fascinated—and still is—by editing and the world of medicine and surgery. Her first hardback, in fact, was a directory of hospitals and clinics, of which she was joint editor. After several years as a medical secretary in London hospitals and in general practice, she went to a voluntary medical organisation as Associate Editor. Here she was also responsible for arranging programmes in the UK for postgraduate doctors and nurses from overseas.

In addition to writing she enjoys pottering about in boats, reading, walking, listening to music, cooking in a slapdash way and trying to keep up with her garden overlooking Richmond Park. She is a former Chairman of the Romantic Novelists' Association.

A Surgeon at St Mark's is Elizabeth Harrison's sixth Doctor Nurse Romance for Mills & Boon; her previous titles include *Marrying a Doctor*, *Surgeon's Affair* and *A Doctor Called Caroline*.

A SURGEON
AT ST MARK'S

BY

ELIZABETH HARRISON

MILLS & BOON LIMITED
15-16 BROOK'S MEWS
LONDON W1A 1DR

First published in Great Britain 1986 by Mills & Boon Limited

© Elizabeth Harrison 1986

Australian copyright 1986 Philippine copyright 1986

ISBN 0 263 75671 8

Set in Linotron Times 10 on 10.5 pt. 03-0287-50204

Typeset in Great Britain by Associated Publishing Services Printed and bound in Great Britain by Collins, Glasgow

CHAPTER ONE

Accident Theatre

'ANOTHER motorcyclist bites the dust,' the staff nurse on the line from the accident unit in the Central London Hospital informed Alix Rutherford in the operating theatre. 'Knocked down by a car coming out of the Euston underpass. Coming up to you as soon as he's had his pre-medication.'

'Major injuries?'

'Mostly to the lower half of the body, Sister. Fracture right femur, compound fracture right tib and fib, and multiple abrasions.'

'I'll need a fracture bed from the ward, then.' Alix was making notes as she spoke. It would be a long job, and once again she could say goodbye to lunch, though this was hardly unusual, as for six months now she'd been junior Sister in the Central's operating theatres. In other words, the dogsbody, at everyone's call at any time of the day or night. Holiday relief, stand-in for sickness or staff shortages, lent at five minutes' notice to any theatre with a problem. None of this worried her at all—she thrived on it. From the day she'd stepped through the doors as a young student nurse, gowned for the first time and shaking with nerves, she'd loved theatre work.

'Another point,' the staff nurse was saying. 'He was wearing a crash helmet, and just as well, but even so he was knocked unconscious. Came round in the ambulance, and neurological observations have remained stable—'

'No cerebral function changes?'

'Not as far as we can tell. But they've decided that in the circumstances they can't risk a general, so they'll be going ahead under a local. Mr Trowbridge is doing it himself, with his registrar and houseman. All right?'

'Fine. We'll be ready for them,' Alix assured her.

It was just after midday when Adam Trowbridge, a stocky powerful man, the orthopaedic surgeon who was director of the accident unit at the Central, came striding into the theatre, gowned and masked, with his house surgeon, Roger Vernon. David Hurst, his registrar, was there already, preparing the patient.

Adam Trowbridge nodded to Alix. 'Morning, Sister. Ready for me? Good. What I propose to do first is to pin the tibia, with Roger here, while David deals with the other injuries. All straightforward?'

'Thank you, sir, yes. I'm ready. And the ward are sending down a traction bed for you.'

Alix was tiny, with dark hair that clung to her small skull, and huge speaking grey eyes. She was also blazingly efficient, and more than due for promotion, they all agreed—indeed, this afternoon she had an appointment to see the Principal Nursing Officer, and it was widely forecast that she was about to be made Sister General Theatres. Stella Bridge, the present holder of the post, was going to retire into private life and bring up a family. She'd told Alix so herself, adding that if Alix wanted the job, she ought to have it.

Alix did want it. More, at the moment, than anything or anyone in the world. Her love life was fading fast—she and David were on the way out, and they both knew it. Here he was in the theatre now, for instance, but she felt nothing.

Theatre staff were routinely bowled over by David Hurst, she knew. She was not the first, and she certainly wouldn't be the last. Perhaps it was like measles. You had it, and then you were immune. As she seemed to be.

David was tall and fair, with handsome sculptured features, close-cut curling hair, and immense charm, that he spread around as easily as he slapped wet plaster on a broken limb, Alix suspected. She had been taken in by all this, and imagined herself to be in love.

Instead it had been infatuation. On both sides, she admitted fairly. And now it was over.

If anything, David had gone off her faster than she had off him, which was very likely, she thought honestly, why she was so exasperated.

'You aren't a bit like I thought you'd be,' he'd told her early on. 'You look so sexy, but inside you're—' he searched for a word.

'Frigid,' she'd supplied, her lip curling.

'No, of course not.' Though she failed to recognise it, he was fundamentally kind, and he hadn't set out to demoralise her. Simply to have a good grumble about her inadequacies. 'Rigid,' he suggested. 'And uptight—like now. If you'd just let yourself go for once. But you're always disciplined. And conscientious.'

'Perhaps you ought to look for a girl-friend among the unemployed,' she'd retorted acidly. She knew she was being unfair, but to fail with him was hard to take. He'd found her, to put it bluntly—not that he ever had—not worth the trouble. The fact that she felt exactly the same was not a lot of help, especially as their failure was played out in front of an attentive audience—Alix was only too well aware that as David's current girl-friend she'd been watched and envied. There was an eager queue ready to take her place, if she failed to make the grade—which was how they would see it.

Well, at least one of the minor advantages of the new post in the general theatre would be that she'd hardly see him. They'd be able to separate unobtrusively, with no hard feelings. Put it down to experience, and turn over the page. Forget David Hurst.

Adam Trowbridge was teaching the students gathered to watch the surgery. He enumerated the measures taken so far. 'Our initial diagnosis has been confirmed by X-rays, and other X-rays reveal no chest or abdominal injuries.' He shot a question out of the blue at his house surgeon, a habit of his. 'Transfusion arrangements?'

Roger was used to him, and ready. 'His blood's been matched and grouped, and two litres are to hand, plenty more next door. I gave him two mega units of penicillin an hour ago.'

'To combat any infection from the open wounds,' Adam explained. 'Now, you can see he's drowsy. Any suggestions as to why?'

'Because he's been concussed?' one of the students ventured.

'Anything else?'

'He must have had pre-medication, sir.' Another student got it right.

'Exactly. That's the reason. His drowsiness will be beneficial.' He turned to the patient. 'Are you fairly happy, laddie?'

'Yes, thanks, Doc. I feel slightly drunk, as a matter of fact.'

'That's OK. I'm going to put a little rod into the top of your leg, here, and this will serve as the point from which we shall apply traction and weights, to straighten your leg, as I was explaining earlier. It'll take quite a bit of time—it's a fiddly sort of job—but quite straightforward. Nothing to worry about. All right?'

Dutifully, the dazed patient agreed it was all OK by him, thanks, Doc, and the operation began. Alix was in her element. This was the sort of session she enjoyed. She kept her head, served them impeccably, and felt her spirits rise by the minute. A well-spent morning. Or, by now, afternoon. She was using her own skills. The surgeons were using theirs. Afterwards the motorcyclist would go to the ward, and the outcome of all their efforts would be his eventual discharge and return to his normal way of life. She was proud to be part of the team that would achieve this—proud, too, that her training had at last brought her to this point. She could run an operating theatre in her teaching hospital.

At last the porters brought the traction bed from the ward, and the patient was lifted on to it. It had overhead beams from which to hang the pulleys carrying the traction cords, and Adam Trowbridge began to arrange the system so that it pulled with the right force and direction to bring the alignment of the broken bone back to normal. It was a long process, and he explained as he went along to both the patient and the students what he was doing and why.

'Why is he tipped up like this?' he asked.

One of the students was prompt. 'So that the patient's own body-weight, sliding with the bed, acts as counter-traction.'

'Quite so. Good. There are now, as you can all see, two forces acting in opposition pulling the two segments of the femur into the correct position. So there you are, laddie,' he told the patient. 'You've done well. Stood up to all this excellently. Off you go, up to the ward—you'll be able to see your parents, I think, they should be waiting there for you by now—and I'll come along and have another look at you a bit later on.' He nodded to Alix. 'Thank you, Sister. Everything's gone very smoothly, but I realise the organisation you've put into it to achieve this—I'm sorry to hear this is our final session. You're leaving us today to go on holiday, is that it?'

'That's right, sir.' David must have told him.

'Enjoy yourself, then. Going anywhere exciting?'

'No, only home—on the coast, though.'

'Get some sun and fresh air, anyway, I dare say. And catch up on your sleep. Oh, and by the way, best of luck with your appointment this afternoon. Hope we haven't made you late for it?'

'No, I still have quarter of an hour in hand.'

'Good. I'll be off, then, out of your way.' He departed in the direction of the surgeons' rest room, followed by David and Roger. The students drifted away, while the porters removed the patient and the traction bed, with the anaesthetist in attendance.

'Imagine him remembering your appointment.' Alix's staff nurse was impressed. 'You haven't much time, though. Why don't you go straight off and change, while I see to clearing up here?'

'Thanks, I'd be grateful if you would.'

'Scarper, then, Sister, stat. And I'll keep my fingers crossed for the new post.'

David himself, gowned, his mask hanging, reappeared. 'Oh, good, I've caught you. Just wanted to say best of luck for the interview and the new post, and have a terrific holiday.'

'Thanks, I will.' Alix was only too well aware that the rest of them in the theatre were watching the encounter raptly.

'See you, then.' He turned back towards the coffee no doubt cooling in the surgeons' rest room. Adoring eyes watched him depart, though Alix's were not among them. So much for David, she was thinking. See you around, he might as well have proclaimed.

Look out for me on the tops of buses, she would have liked to retort. Frowning—maybe she was immune to him, but suddenly it seemed lonely out there all by herself again—she went off to change, turning her attention firmly towards presenting herself as perfect departmental Sister material. She put on the dark blue dress, her state-registered belt with its intricate silver buckle, did her hair so that it lay smoothly under the crisp white cap with its sister's bows, made up her face afresh—not too much, not too little—and presented herself punctually at the office.

'Come in, Miss Rutherford.' The Principal Nursing Officer was welcoming. 'Sit down. Coffee?'

The full treatment. So it was in the bag, just as they had all assured her. 'Thank you, I'd love some.'

Miss Frobisher poured from the gleaming silver pot, and afterwards made the forecast offer. Alix, to neither of their surprise, accepted it. They discussed her salary, holiday entitlement, possible staff changes in the general theatres in the year ahead. Miss Frobisher reminded her that as a departmental Sister, there would be a fair number of committees on which she would be expected to sit. There was, it seemed, a price to be paid for everything, and this was the price for taking on the post of Sister General Theatres. Committees. Alix thought she'd be able to bear it.

Walking on air—she really was amazingly pleased—she left the hospital and returned to her flat, to change yet again, this time into jeans and a sweater and her anorak. She caught her train comfortably, and arrived at Halchester in the gathering dusk.

Her father was to meet her there, but there was no sign of him. Daniel Rutherford had never had any sense of time. Alix settled herself down on a bench in the booking hall where she could keep an eye on the forecourt, and took out her magazine again. Impossible to guess whether her father was merely late, or whether he'd forgotten about meeting her. She'd give him a quarter of an hour.

She heard the bell signalling the approach of the London train, and at the same moment her father's silver Porsche drew up in the forecourt. Thankfully, Alix stowed her magazine and made for the car.

Her father must have had a passenger. A bulky man in a formal city suit came fast through the entrance on his way to the ticket office. Brought by her father, and about to miss the London train, obviously. Typical. He would have knocked Alix off her feet in his rush, except that somehow he managed to catch her and hold her securely in two strong and curiously reassuring arms. 'My fault,' he said shortly, dark eyes under heavy brows scanning not Alix but the station clock. 'So sorry. All right?' His arms might feel reassuring, but his voice was curt, and clearly implied that she had better be.

'Quite all right, thank you.' Alix disengaged herself, more than a little astonished by a weird inner reluctance to do anything of the sort. What could be so special about this abrupt stranger? Nothing at all.

He nodded, and headed for the ticket office, while Alix joined her father.

He wasn't looking well—he was a bad colour, and wheezing, too. Evidently his bronchitis had started early this year. However, his poor colour didn't necessarily mean anything. Indoors all day and every day, taking no exercise, instead reading, making innumerable notes or pounding his typewriter, he often had the pallid look of an over-tried house surgeon who seldom if ever breathed real outdoor air. He worked much the same hours, too, though the demands in his case came only from himself. He was the author of best-selling thrillers, as well as of a series of history textbooks for secondary schools, from both of which activities he made a more than adequate income.

He kissed Alix. 'Sorry to be late. Good game of chess, and I'm afraid we both forgot the time. Been waiting long?'

'Not very. Doesn't matter. Who was your stampeding passenger? Caught the London train by the skin of his teeth.'

'Oh, that was Jo Standish. He's fairly new to the district, so you wouldn't have met him.'

'I thought he must be someone from your publishers, as he was dashing for the London train. Nearly knocked me down in his rush.'

'Did he? No, he's not from Wingfield Press. He lives down here—he was going up to London for some conference or other. He's in your line, as it happens. Surgeon at St Mark's Hospital.'

That accounted for it. The expensive suit, the get-out-of-my-way-or-else attitude, the unpunctuality and the turn of speed when it was needed. And the brusqueness. Recognisable surgical behaviour.

'Not at all a bad chess player.' Her father's voice cut across Alix's thoughts. 'I have to push myself hard to beat him—though I usually manage to.'

This was quite something. Finding a local partner of his own calibre had always been a problem.

'Apparently he's rather an acquisition for St Mark's—they reckon they're lucky to have landed him. So Basil Lomax was telling me. Oh, never mind that now, though. What's your news?'

'Rather good.' Alix had been looking forward to telling her father about her new post. 'I'm to be Sister General Theatres.'

'Glad to hear it.' Daniel's voice was abstracted as he negotiated the entry to the motorway and crossed into the fast lane. 'What you wanted, is it?'

She ought to have been prepared for this vagueness,

but she wasn't. Sometimes she doubted whether he even knew exactly where it was she worked, and certainly the details of her career remained a closed book to him. However, she reminded herself, she had no right to blame him. She on her side understood nothing of his life as a writer, other than the fact that it caused him to shut himself away in his room, ignore her and everyone else, and forget the time.

They were off the motorway now, driving down the lane to Field End. Originally two adjoining cottages, discovered derelict and empty by Daniel Rutherford when he was a young history master at the grammar school, over the intervening years they had been improved and enlarged, and now the ground floor was one huge room, with a big open fireplace one end, a door into the quarry-tiled kitchen with its Aga at the other, while where the party wall had once been a staircase of gleaming elm climbed to a balconied landing.

Field End looked out across fields towards the sea, and was sheltered from the cold north winds by the wooded hillside behind. The casement windows with their leaded panes were double-glazed, and today the cottage was comfortable as well as beautiful. Extensive, too—ten years earlier, while Alix was still at school, Daniel had also built on a garage block, with a writing room upstairs, where he could shut himself away from the telephone and any callers.

'Can you manage your stuff?' he enquired, as he pulled up in the garage. 'Or shall I help you in with it?'

'No, I'll be fine, Dad. I haven't brought much with me.' She knew exactly what was coming next.

It came. 'I'll leave you, then. Want to get back to the book. I think Woody said she'd left you something in the oven. 'Night, dear. Nice to have you back. See you in the morning, I expect.' He began to mount the stairs leading from the garage lobby up to his writing room.

Alix turned towards the kitchen entrance. And welcome home to you, too, she thought, disappointed. Couldn't he have spared even ten minutes for a drink and a chat?

Of course he couldn't. He never had and he never would. His writing came first, last, and everywhere in between. That was the sort of man he was. To imagine he might suddenly have changed was ridiculous.

Probably she was hungry, and a bit tired, and that was what was making her cross and demanding. She'd find Woody's supper in the oven and have her meal.

Woody, their housekeeper, lived down the lane with her husband, Sam, who ran the local taxi service. Her cooking was conventional, but what she produced melted in the mouth, and the shepherd's pie waiting in the oven proved no exception. There were fresh blackberries, too, with a jug of cream, and then Alix made coffee, her earlier depression vanished, her thoughts centred, excitedly and hopefully, on her future management of the general theatres.

She took her case upstairs to her bedroom. Her father, though detached and lost in his own world most of the year, could give wonderful presents. Alix's bedroom had been one of them. After the garage block had been completed, he'd had two of the small bedrooms upstairs in the cottage itself knocked into one long room, with windows looking out towards the sea at one end and over the woodland at the other. This, he had informed a stunned and delighted Alix, was to be her own study-bedroom. She could furnish it how she liked. 'Just choose what you want—consult your Aunt Zoe about it.'

With Zoe, sister of the mother she could hardly any longer remember, Alix had searched through

Halchester's antique shops, emerging with a chest of drawers, a small desk and a little heart-shaped mirror. Zoe had contributed flowery chintz curtains and divan cover, together with a charming little Victorian armchair, and Sam had made a low bookshelf under the window.

Slipping into bed, she looked happily round. What would her father's reaction be, she wondered, if she proposed, now that she had a permanent post at the Central, finding an unfurnished flat and moving her bedroom furniture into it—lock, stock and barrel?

Probably he wouldn't care one way or the other, she decided, and began planning a small and delightful flat of her own, round the corner from the hospital, where, as she drifted off to sleep, she seemed to be serving supper to someone she recognised at once, in spite of his highly improbable garb of surgical gown and mask, as the giant who had all but knocked her down at the station.

CHAPTER TWO

A Talk With Dr Lomax

IN the morning, Alix slept on until Woody woke her with a tray of coffee, scrambled egg and two crisp rashers of bacon, plus toast and home-made marmalade. 'Here's your breakfast, Alix. I thought you'd better have a bit of a lie-in now you're down here—you're sure to have been working too hard and getting far too little sleep, same as your dad. Two of a kind, you are. Your aunt rang, and said to tell you she'd expect you straight after lunch. She's in the middle of a play, and she's relying on you to help her.'

Like Alix's mother, her aunt Zoe was an actress, but instead of disappearing to Hollywood and the big time, she'd married a Halchester businessman, and made the little open-air theatre in the garden of her house on the cliffs her main preoccupation. If the weather let her down, as it often did, she opened the house to players and audience, and in any case she provided dressing rooms as well as a bar and buffet. Often she herself was producer, casting director, wardrobe mistress and stage manager. She worked the cast into the ground, and bullied them tyrannically. There were always rows, recriminations and tempestuous partings, but her actors and actresses nearly always came back, and Zoe herself seemed to thrive on the uproar.

'What's the play, do you know?'

17

'Search me.' Neither Zoe nor the theatre were among Woody's passions. 'Some modern piece or other,' she said dismissively. 'Anyway, as soon as she heard you'd be at home this week, she said you must go over and help her. I said you'd want to have lunch with your dad—after all it *is* your first day here—so she said go over straight afterwards, stay for tea and supper, and work on the play with her.'

Typical Zoe, dictatorial as usual. However, her productions were fun as well as hard work, and on the whole Alix was pleased to join her. Holidays at Field End would have been lonely without her, and plainly this one would have been no exception. She'd be lucky if she saw her father for an hour or two a day, at the midday meal.

'Steak and kidney pie for lunch,' Woody said, pausing at the door of her room. 'I won't leave you any supper, though, as you'll be having it with your aunt. Oh, and Dr Lomax wants to see you.'

'What on earth for?' Alix was astounded.

'That's what he said, Alix. You'd better go over before lunch, get it done with.'

What on earth could Dr Lomax want to see her for? Surely now she was at the Central he didn't imagine he had to watch over her still? Light dawned. He did. He was a conscientious family doctor, he'd known her all her life, and he wanted to check up that she was eating and sleeping properly, hadn't lost weight, and hadn't missed out on any of her jabs.

Alix ran downstairs in jeans and trainers, and, to celebrate the beginning of the holiday, her favourite shirt. Ten minutes walk only to the big Edwardian house where Lomax, Burbidge and Singh held their twice daily surgeries, and where Dr Lomax and his family lived. She went into the familiar hall, and nodded to the receptionist, whom she'd often assisted during her school holidays before she began her nursing training—it had been Dr Lomax, a Central man himself, who'd sent her to her teaching hospital. 'Morning, Hilary,' she said cheerfully. 'Dr Lomax wanted me to look in, Mrs. Woods said.'

Hilary, usually matey, gave her a guarded look. 'He's expecting you, that's right,' she agreed. 'I'll just tell him you're here.'

Alix was surprised. Usually she announced herself. What was more, Hilary didn't simply put her head round the door, saying, 'Alix is here, shall I send her in?' Instead she went through the door, shutting it firmly behind her.

When she came out she was followed by Drs Burbidge and Singh, carrying their coffee with them and adjourning, apparently, to Dr Burbidge's room to drink it. 'Morning, Alix,' Dr Burbidge greeted her. But he avoided her eyes, while Dr Singh gave her, in his turn, a quick nod and a hunted look.

What was going on?

'I'll bring you some coffee,' Hilary said. 'Go straight in now.'

'Come in, Alix. Sit down, my dear. I want to talk to you.'

Hilary reappeared, with coffee on a tray. The best visitors' china, Alix noted automatically. She'd gone up in the world. Chocolate biscuits, too.

'I'm sorry to have to break into your holiday like this,' Dr Lomax said.

'Like what?'

'Has your father said anything to you yet?'

'Dad? What about?'

Dr Lomax sighed. 'I was afraid he wouldn't have done, though I asked him to. However, you have to know, as I told him. My dear, I'm afraid he's not at all well. Rather poorly, in fact.'

'Poorly?' It was an ominous word. At the Central it usually meant they thought the patient might very likely die. '*Dad*? Well, I noticed he was a bad colour last night, and he was wheezing again, but—'

'Yes, you're right, it's his chest, as usual. But this time I'm afraid it's serious. He's had several haemoptyses.'

Alix didn't know what exactly she had been expecting, but that her father might be so ill he was coughing up blood hadn't occurred to her. 'Several haemoptyses?' she repeated, hardly able to take it in.

'Yes. Mrs Wood kept finding these bloody handkerchiefs. Blood on his shirts, too. He refused to discuss it. She tried to make him come and see me, but he kept putting her off, saying he'd come when his book was finished, that sort of thing.'

Alix nodded. 'How he always is.'

'So in the end I called in one afternoon on my rounds, and tackled him about it.'

'What did he say?'

'That it was nothing, Mrs Wood was a fuss-pot, and if I insisted he'd have an overhaul when he'd finished his book. Eventually, however, he told me what had been happening. He's been coughing more than usual—more than usual for the summer, that is.' Daniel Rutherford had always had a bad chest. As an asthmatic child, he'd been sent away to school in Switzerland, but except for a brief recurrence during his short and unhappy marriage, he'd grown out of his asthma, though he remained liable to nasty attacks of bronchitis every winter.

'I suppose he didn't think of cutting down his smoking or anything like that?'

'Not while he's writing,' Dr Lomax replied, as Alix had known he would. Her father's bronchitis was always made worse by smoking—even as a schoolgirl she'd seen cause and effect for herself, and badgered him to stop. He did make sporadic attempts to cut down, but never when he had a book under way.

Some years ago, she'd persuaded him to change the cigarettes he chain-smoked for small cigars, but that had been his only concession.

'Anyway,' Dr Lomax told her, 'I made him let me examine him, and when I listened to his chest, I got persistent bronchial breathing in the right upper lobe. It didn't seem to me to fit a simple flare-up of his bronchitis, and I hoped it might be a patch of pneumonitis that would settle, but I decided he ought to have a chest picture. He refused. No time, he said. So in the end I simply made an appointment for him, and went along and took him to the X-ray department at St Marks'.'

'Terrific of you.'

'And now I have the radiologist's report.' Dr Lomax sighed, and fiddled uneasily with the papers on his desk. 'It's not good news, my dear. There's a shadow in the area where I heard the bronchial breathing.'

'A growth, you mean?' Putting her fear into words made it more real, and an arctic chill seemed to spread through her bones.

'No use pretending I don't think that's what it is. Dr Parsons—he's the radiologist at St Mark's now—isn't certain as to its nature, and wants your father to have tomograms, but Daniel won't hear of it. In any case, though, Dr Parsons doesn't think we'll get the answer by radiology—he says full investigation will have to follow.'

Alix found her mouth had dried. She drank some coffee and tried to assemble her thoughts.

Dr Lomax watched her with kindly, worried eyes. 'I'm so sorry, my dear. I hate confronting you with all this when you've come down for a short holiday. But I came to the conclusion you simply had to know. It's providential you're here at the moment, because if you and I both have a go at him, we ought to be able to get him investigated. And frankly I think delay could be dangerous.'

Alix looked him straight in the eye. 'Do you think he has lung cancer?'

'Who can say? We have to hope it isn't—and of course there's a chance it may not be—but we have to recognise it's undoubtedly one of the possibilities. I sent off his sputum to the path lab at St Mark's for cells, but they didn't find anything. For what it's worth.'

'No malignant cells?'

'None.' He shrugged. 'That doesn't mean they aren't there, though. They often can't find them. That doesn't clear him.'

'No, I realise that,' Alix said. 'What do you see as the next step, then, apart from the tomograms— which I'll somehow see he has while I'm at home. If I don't achieve anything else, I'll get him to the X-ray department again.'

'I'd like him to see a surgeon. I thought we might get that moving while you're here, too.'

Alix nodded. 'Certainly. Who were you thinking of?' Her mind travelled rapidly over the thoracic consultants at the Central.

'I have someone local in mind,' Dr Lomax said, a good deal to her surprise. 'We have a new young consultant here. Only just been appointed.'

If her father was going to need surgery, it was simply not good enough for him to see some newly-appointed local nobody, and Alix opened her mouth to say so, and then clamped it shut again. A local man might offer the only hope of getting him to see anyone before his book was finished—and when would that be? The other side of Christmas, very likely. Months away, and he might have a fast-growing lung cancer that would spread.

Dr Lomax read her mind. 'I know how you feel,

my dear. What I'd like myself would be to have him
thoroughly investigated at the Central. It was my first
thought. But your father wouldn't hear of it. If he
had to see anyone, it must be someone local—and I
rather think that was only because, by the mercy of
God, before all this blew up, I'd already introduced
them, and your father liked him. So he seemed to
think he might just find sufficient time away from his
book to discuss the problem, but that's his limit.'

'What do you think his chances are?'

'I'd like to say fifty-fifty, my dear. But I'm afraid
that would be over-optimistic. More like three to one
against him.'

Alix swallowed. 'And you do truly think this local
man is the right one? I mean, not just to see him and
have a consultation, but to go ahead and operate, if
that's what it comes to?'

'He's the right man now.' Dr Lomax was emphatic.
'He's a Central man, anyway, originally. Now he's
been appointed thoracic surgeon here, with special
responsibility for the accident unit—they've made him
deputy director, to take some of the load off the
director.'

'And you really do think he's good?'

'I do. Plus the fact that he knows your father, and
they get on well. Play chess together.'

Alix felt her jaw drop. She hauled it back in.
'What's his name?' she enquired faintly.

'Standish. Jo Standish. I'm hoping—'

'Dad mentioned him to me yesterday. Certainly he
seemed to like him, I agree.' And I like him too.
This revealing and utterly unexpected phrase almost
popped out of Alix's mouth before she could stop it,
but she bit it back just in time, astonished at herself.
How could she possibly know whether she liked this
Standish man or not? The only fact she had to go on
was that he charged round Halchester ready to knock

down anyone who stood in his way. He has a nice face, a voice inside her remarked clearly. And arms like oak trees. You could be safe with him for ever.

What a ludicrous idea. She wrenched her attention back to Dr Lomax, whom she did know, who'd looked after her for years. He was the one she should be turning to, not this madman who tried to trample her down.

'We must plan a campaign,' Dr Lomax said. 'I'd like you to have a talk with Jo Standish, as a start, and he promised me he'd look in here tomorrow before evening surgery, so that we could have a consultation about your father. I'd like you to be here too, if you can.'

'Of course I can.' To talk to Jo Standish was a gleam of light in her suddenly darkened world.

'Half an hour before surgery, then. I'll expect you.'

'I'll be here,' Alix promised. She frowned. 'Do you—ought I to say anything to Dad today, do you think?'

Dr Lomax patted her hand. 'The news has been a shock to you, my dear. Naturally. Think around it a bit before you talk to Daniel, would be my advice. Come along here again tomorrow, and we'll all three of us thrash it out, formulate some sort of policy. Until then I'd lie low.'

'I'd much rather wait. I don't feel I have the slightest idea what to say to him, or what to do.' She heard the quiver in her voice, and was furious with herself. What had happened to cool, calm, unflappable Alix Rutherford, newly appointed Sister General Theatres, who could handle anything that came up without turning a hair? Vanished without trace, leaving only a frightened panicking girl without the slightest notion of how to handle a dangerously ill parent.

'I'm sorry, Alix. I didn't want to involve you in all

this, but there seemed no alternative. Daniel has no one else. Only you.'

He had no one else. It was the truth. Her mother was two marriages and nearly twenty years away. Alix was his next of kin. And what was more, she reminded herself irritably, she was a trained nurse. A silver medallist from the Central. A senior sister at a teaching hospital ready to take charge in any emergency. So pull yourself together, Alix Rutherford. This is an emergency, and you're the one to handle it. Get cracking. Cope.

She walked back to Field End, and succeeded in eating lunch with her father without letting him guess that she knew how ill he might be. She studied him carefully, though, with a keen and clinical eye. He was a bad colour, as she'd noticed yesterday, and he was breathless, with an undoubted wheeze. He had very little appetite, either, picking round Woody's steak and kidney pie and leaving most of it, so that Alix felt her own voracious appetite out of place. He refused cheese, ate one or two grapes, and then, to Alix's fury, lit one of his pungent cigars and smoked it with his coffee.

She held on to her temper. If they were going, between them, to persuade him to be treated, to begin by ordering him to stop smoking would be asking for trouble.

He caught her eye, gave her a sheepish grin. 'I know exactly what you're thinking.'

Alix crossed her fingers and hoped he had no idea.

'But I enjoy a cigar after a morning's writing, and I'm damned if I'm going to give up smoking, for you or anyone else.'

Anyone else? Had Dr Lomax been on to him? Or could it possibly have been Jo Standish?

'Going to your aunt's this afternoon, are you?'

'That's right. To help her with the last play of the season.'

'Take the Porsche. I shan't want it.'

Reluctantly Alix turned down this unprecedented offer. 'It's all right, thanks, Dad. I'll walk. I need the exercise.' What she needed was time. Time to try, if not to come to terms with what Dr Lomax had told her, at least to work out where she stood, what they were going to have to do about her father.

She'd go along the cliff path. Think things out. There were no actual decisions to be made yet, she reminded herself. Far too early for that. In fact, what she had to do was to calm herself down.

But she might be going to lose her father. Unseeing, she stared down towards the jagged rocks at the foot of the cliff, and then out to sea. She might be going to lose her father within a few months.

She had to do something. He mustn't be allowed to throw his life away simply because he was too interested in his current book to spare an hour or two—or even a week or two—to be investigated and treated.

They had to find out exactly how bad he was, if there was anything that could be done before it was too late. And it was up to her. She was the only one. Somehow she had to force sense into him. He had no one else.

No good consulting Zoe. She was a poppet, and enormous fun. Her advice on what to wear and how to put on make-up was well worth having. But she knew nothing about medicine, she and Daniel didn't get on, and, most dangerous of all, she couldn't keep her mouth shut.

If she heard about Daniel's illness, her first reaction would be to rush round telling the whole of Halchester, and her second to bombard him with a series of plans that would be bound, she was sure, to cure him in no time. Like eating the latest vegetarian diet, or consulting this fantastic astrologer.

Miserably, Alix plodded on along the cliff, deaf to the crying of the gulls wheeling and turning above the tide, blind to the sky above and the sea below.

What needed to be done had to be done by her. And after all, she had the best possible support. Professional. Dr Lomax, and Mr Jo Standish.

Jo Standish, of the warm supporting arms, and the bleak and distant voice.

She set her lips. There it was. She had the two of them.

CHAPTER THREE

The Cliff-Top Theatre

ALIX opened the wicket gate that led from the cliff
path into Zoe's beautifully kept garden, where she
had created her open-air theatre, sat down on one of
the stone benches, and listened to the tide surging
and crashing at the base of the cliffs. In this fragrant
sunny spot, with the wind in her hair and the sun
glinting on the water, the possibility that her father
might be dying seemed no more than an incredible
rumour.

Yet it was the truth.

Suddenly she grasped what it was she had to do,
and saw inescapably what her first step must be. She
had to stay with him at Field End. No getting away
from it. It wouldn't be enough, whatever Dr Lomax
might kindly imply, to put in an appearance for a
brief fortnight, and, duty done, clear off thankfully to
the Central and her new job.

She had to be there, looking after him. She couldn't
disappear and leave his care to some private nurse
that an agency would find for Dr. Lomax. Nor could
she allow her father to be admitted for months on
end to one of Halchester's top nursing homes, no
matter how excellent it might be. She was trained
and capable. She had to stay here with him.

She had to.

From the house Zoe caught sight of her, a slight
figure, dark hair ruffled by the wind, in washed-out

jeans and a pale pink shirt. She leant out of the study window, where she was working on her lists for the opening night, waving and calling out cheerfully.

Alix jumped up, walked across the lawn and into the house to join her.

'There you are, dear. I thought you looked a bit sad and lonely, there on the seat. That's why I called you in. Has anything happened?'

Oh *no*. Surely she couldn't be as obvious as that? 'Heavens, no. I expect I was a bit flaked—I walked over, along the cliffs.'

Zoe shuffled her lists into a neat pile. 'Then we'll have tea, and afterwards I'll go through these with you. I can't tell you how glad I am you're home— when you're here for one of my performances you lift a load off my shoulders always. I know I can rely on you to spot anything I've forgotten, and deal with it.'

How nice. She must pull herself together and concentrate, otherwise Zoe would pick up her anxiety and realise she'd been right the first time. Something was very wrong indeed. So for the next five hours, in addition to consuming a vast tea followed by a huge dinner, Alix worked with Zoe on her lists, until finally, her mind spinning, she returned to Field End, fell into bed, and slept. Zoe wanted her back early the next day, to help with the dress rehearsal. 'I'll need you. There's bound to be some disaster. There always is.'

There was. When Alix arrived, Zoe was on the telephone. She put the receiver down with an impatient clatter. 'That was Tessa's mother. The stupid girl had to go out jogging as usual this morning, wouldn't you know, and she's tripped and sprained her ankle.'

To Alix it seemed a minor problem. 'She doesn't come on until the very end, does she? Can't I walk on for her today? It's a very brief appearance, after all.'

'That's true. You're always level-headed, dear. That ought to be fine.'

'And afterwards we can work something out.'

Alix spoke too soon.

'I've already worked it out dear, thanks to you. You can do it. Every performance.'

'But I—'

'You don't have to say anything, simply walk across the stage and back.' Zoe had learnt the hard way, organising the Halchester pageant in her early days, that amateur actors, speaking in the open air, could rarely be heard. The plays she put on nowadays were pre-recorded, the actors miming their parts. The results were amazingly effective, and audiences flocked to her productions. 'It'll be much easier for me to give you a quick coaching than anyone else,' she assured Alix confidently. 'Nothing to it. Pop along to the dressing rooms and try on Tessa's gear for the part.'

This proved to be a lurid magenta sweater topped by a black leather jacket loaded with studs, chains and evil badges, worn with a brief, slit leather skirt and dangerous spiky-heeled boots. Alix thought she might well have looked fantastic in the outfit, except for the awkward fact that Tessa was obviously twice her size.

Zoe was thrown.

'The jacket might just do,' Alix suggested dubiously.

'Try, anyway. If you wore that, and we did your hair for the part, that would have to do for tonight. After that I'll look something out. Try it on and see.'

Alix put the jacket on, and saw a new personality in the wide dressing room mirror. Tough. Aggressive. 'I've an old pair of purple cords at home, that I've more or less stopped wearing because they're so tight.

They might go quite well with the jacket—I could slip home and get them.'

'Do that.' Zoe was decisive. 'But first I'll do your hair—before the crowd turns up. Sit down.'

Alix sat, Zoe applied mousse and bright purple colour lavishly.

'For heaven's sake,' Alix protested. 'I'm only going to be on for a few minutes—is all this truly essential?'

'It's a few minutes that brings the curtain down, don't forget. And it's the way you look and move that does it. You must strut about and waggle your hips, but at the same moment manage to look thoroughly tough and couldn't care less. You're joining this fearfully upper-class family as the new daughter-in-law they've all been waiting for, married to their stinking rich tycoon of a son who's going to pay off their debts and reroof the mouldering old pile. You have to shock them out of their minds— and the audience at the same moment. Forget your inhibitions. Just remember you're meant to be fairly horrible and bursting with aggro, and let it surge out all over you. There you are, that's your hair done.'

Alix stared, shaken, at her new image. A tough little cookie with nothing to learn, who could make her own way anywhere. She looked, suddenly, what she never felt. Streetwise.

'Now let's see you walk across the room,' Zoe ordered. 'Come on, girl, move. Swing your shoulders and stick your bottom out. Your lower lip, too. She drew a quick astonished breath. 'You're going to be great, Alix. I believe in you myself, almost.'

'I'll fetch my purple jeans, then, and leave it at that, shall I?'

'Plus a pair of spiky shoes, if you can lay hands on them. Off you go. Don't hang about, will you? I want you back here to help me with the cast as soon as you can make it.'

Driving through Halchester in the Porsche with her purple hair and Tessa's black leather jacket, Alix for the first time felt she had a personality to match the car. She was an angry pop star, driving her own powerful machine, she was loaded, and she cared nothing for anyone. She swung the car into Field End's drive, turned it round ready for the return to Zoe's, gravel spurting, and only then remembered who she was and what was really happening in her life. Impatiently she shook her purple head. The play was a welcome break in the gloom, gave her something different to think about for a day or two, and she was going to enjoy it.

She didn't even pause to wonder whose was the big Volvo parked by the front door.

In the large living-room, though, her father looked up from the chess board, and his partner glanced up with him. He was, of course, Jo Standish.

Alix, halfway across the room on her way upstairs, noticed nothing. 'Good afternoon, Mr Standish.' She was as formal as if she'd been on a Central teaching round, and forgot how inappropriate her get-up was for such an occasion. 'Don't stop playing on my account, Dad,' she added. As if he would. 'I'm just collecting some stuff and going straight back to Zoe's.'

'Fine. Enjoy yourself.' Her father returned to his next move and, immersed in his game, failed to spot his partner's stunned reaction to the purple hair and leather jacket disappearing along the balcony.

Alix went to her room to hunt for the purple cords, and tried them on. By holding her stomach taunt as a drum, she was just able to insert herself into them and zip them up. She slammed the cupboard doors, and zoomed downstairs.

Her father didn't look up, but Jo Standish's fascinated gaze followed her every step down the full flight. His expression—he'd had warning, this time round—was unreadable, but his thoughts whirled. Daniel Rutherford was very likely dying, and this was his only relative. This was the girl Dr Lomax had arranged for him to meet this evening. This monstrous creature, uncaring, brazen, heartless, was the assistance that unworldly family doctor imagined he'd called in to support poor Daniel. Jo's lips tightened. She'd be useless. One glance told you that.

When Alix arrived back, the dress rehearsal had begun, and Zoe was immersed in the production.

'There you are at last—check up for me on the Act Three people in the dressing rooms, would you? Don't let any of them stray, for Pete's sake. I want them dressed and made up and on stage inside fifteen minutes. Most of them haven't the slightest sense of time. Chivvy them for me.'

Act Two and the first part of Act Three sped by, as Alix commuted between Zoe and her clipboard in the wings, and the dressing rooms up in the house. In what seemed no time at all she had to position herself for her own entrance.

By now she was hot, tired, and far too rushed to be nervous. Sexily, arrogantly, she strode across the stage, her shoulders going and her chin out, grey eyes gleaming like cold sea-washed pebbles, and radiating similar hardness.

And then the rehearsal was over, and the chattering broke out, only to die away as Zoe stepped forward with her clipboard, pointing an angry jabbing pencil, telling them how terrible they'd been, and where exactly they'd gone wrong.

This post mortem was to be followed by coffee and Danish pastries in the conservatory, but in order to be at Dr Lomax's surgery in time Alix had to skip this.

'Oh, must you go, dear?' Zoe was put out. 'I

thought you'd be staying for supper, and we could go right through my notes together.'

'Frightfully sorry, but I have this appointment, and I'm late already.'

At the surgery Hilary let her in, and did an immediate double-take.

At that point Alix realised she hadn't changed. 'It's the play,' she explained hastily. 'It was getting late, so I came straight here.'

'Oh, that's what it is. I couldn't believe you'd become a new character overnight. In you go, then—they're both here waiting for you, and there's sherry.' She gave Alix a second scrutiny. 'You look as if you could do with it, I must say. Your hair may be ready for take-off, and your outfit, but you look pretty well all in to me. Sure you're all right?'

'I'm fine, thanks, Hilary.'

'In you go, then.' Hilary opened the door of Dr Lomax's consulting room. 'Here she is,' she announced breezily. 'Straight from the latest production of the Cliff Top Theatre, in case you're wondering about her get-up,' she added, as two pairs of bemused male eyes blinked unbelievingly at their visitor.

'Come in, Alix. Sit down and have a glass of sherry, my dear.' Dr Lomax was joviality itself, a habit of his before difficult interviews he dreaded. He settled Alix into the armchair at one side of his big mahogany desk, the chair on the other side already being occupied by Jo Standish, nursing a sherry glass and looking baleful.

Dr Lomax sank back into his own leather-padded desk chair and swung back and forth in it, facing now Alix, now Jo. His eyes twinkled momentarily as he surveyed them, and he chuckled. 'I must say, my dear,' he told Alix, 'you look magnificent.' Unfortunately, he at once undid the effect of this statement by adding, 'And quite unlike your usual self. No wonder Jo here was a bit nonplussed.' He swung round to confront Jo, undoubted mockery in his gaze now.

The surgeon flushed, frowned. 'You'll agree, presumably, that—'

'Oh, I see well enough now what you were driving at. Alix, my dear, Mr Standish'— to the further embarrassment of both his visitors, he chose suddenly to revert to the most formal of nomenclature—'Mr Standish, somewhat to my astonishment, has been telling me he was uneasy about your capacity to cope with the problem of your poor father. I see why now. He'd seen you in your theatrical outfit only, and must have assumed it to be a reflection of your personality.' He twinkled again.

Jo Standish, however, was scowling. He was being made a fool of by the two of them.

Alix reddened. She didn't know what she felt, except that she would very much like to be somewhere else, and in her ordinary clothes. Wearing a headscarf, too. To fill in time, she sipped her sherry, and thankfully a reassuring warmth spread through her amazingly tired limbs. Her mind, however was not tired. Only worried. She was here for a purpose, it wasn't going to be easy to reach some sort of conclusion about her father. What was more, they had to complete their discussion before evening surgery began. 'I should be glad to know what you both think about my father's condition,' she stated coldly, sounding extraordinarily like a senior nursing officer from a teaching hospital quelling two recalcitrant young house surgeons who knew less than nothing about the patients in the ward.

Jo Standish caught the authority of the teaching hospital at once, and not unnaturally, coming from this sexy urchin with hair in purple spikes and skin tight jeans, lolling in her chair like a randy guttersnipe, it astounded him.

Dr Lomax, on the other hand, used to Alix from childhood, ignored her appearance after his one amused remark. To him it was only as though she'd come to talk to him in the middle of playing charades with his own children. However she happened to be dressed, she was the same old Alix. However, he recognised—he could hardly fail to, the air across his desk was icy—that his two visitors were so far ill-adjusted. He took charge and began busily pouring oil on the troubled waters.

'Thank you both for coming in this evening,' he said smoothly. 'It'll take the three of us, I'm afraid, to persuade that obstinate father of yours, Alix, to allow us to do what we can to help him. Now, I explained the position, as I see it, to you the other morning, Alix, and I've already discussed the clinical findings with you, Jo. And of course, luckily you've met Daniel, and you know the sort of chap he is. Would you like to tell Miss Rutherford what you think the next step should be?'

Jo fixed his eyes firmly on the ceiling, so that he could avoid the unsettling, disruptive view of Alix herself, removed all extraneous problems from his mind, and concentration slipped over him as easily as it would have done in the wards. 'Sputum cytology you've done,' he said. 'What we want immediately are tomograms from two angles. Ultimately, though, we have to plan to bronchoscope him. Until we've done that, and seen inside his chest, we can't plan treatment or take a decision as to whether he's going to require surgery.'

'It's not going to be easy to get him to have tomograms, even,' Dr Lomax pointed out. 'As I think I mentioned, I had to call in at Field End and cart him off against his protests for his first X-ray appointment.'

'I'm afraid he's always a bit impossible when he has a book on the stocks.' Alix was apologetic. 'Nothing else exists for him, you see.'

'If he has a growth in his chest, it's not going to stop growing while he finishes his book.' Jo was downright. 'It's in his own interest to be investigated, and the sooner the better.'

'Oh, I agree,' Alix said hastily. 'That's why I'm here, after all.' As soon as the words were out of her mouth she realised she'd been too snappy. She must have sounded as if she was trying to pick a quarrel. Confused, she took refuge again in a teaching hospital formula. 'And why you've been kind enough to spare time to come in to talk about his case, of course,' she added, sounding very grand and distant, and confusing Jo even more than herself.

Dr Lomax stepped in and poured yet more oil. 'Well, I managed to get him to the X-ray department once,' he said cheerfully. 'And now, after all I have reinforcements,'—though it's a pity they seem to hate one another, he thought irritably—'So I dare say between us we can get him there again if we try. After that it'll be a question of the bronchoscopy. That, of course, will be much tougher for him than X-rays, but I'm afraid in the circumstances it's unavoidable, eh Jo?'

'It's essential we should get a look into his chest, certainly. Probably do a biopsy, too.'

'And then, I suppose, you're thinking of a thoracotomy.' Reluctantly, Alix spelled it out. They were sitting here planning to open up her father's chest, and remove part of his lung.

'Inevitably.' Jo was terse. 'If we find what we suspect.'

'Of course, there's always a chance that we may be

mistaken.' Dr Lomax pointed out. 'We must continue to hope that is so.'

'But the hope is slender.' Alix summed it up.

'I'm afraid so.' For the first time, Jo looked at her, and met great sad eyes in a pale exhausted face. So she did care. She was suffering, and genuinely worried to death, even if she did spend her days prancing about dressed outrageously. And she had, after all, come along here tonight straight from this wretched play, whatever it was. He must try to be fair to her. And hope, for Daniel Rutherford's sake, that her more serious side remained uppermost for long enough to help him.

'I must ask,' Alix spoke slowly and deliberately, hating what she was going to say, yet knowing it had to be said, since this, after all, was what they were here for, why Dr Lomax and Jo Standish had given up their free time to meet her. To decide on her father's treatment. So decide they must, however unwelcome the decision. 'I must ask, do you both think he'd be fit for a thoracotomy? I mean, would you bronchoscope him if you were doubtful he'd stand surgery?'

Dr Lomax intervened. 'My dear, we can face that problem when we know whether he needs one. Our first step, after all, is to—'

'No,' Jo said. 'It's a good question.' This damned girl had startled him again. This was a point he would have expected Dr Lomax himself to raise, not this gaudy creature with purple hair, even if she had somehow succeeded in completing a nursing training at the Central. Or so Lomax asserted. 'I wouldn't want to subject any patient to a bronchoscopy,' he said, addressing the ceiling again, 'unless there was something to be gained from the procedure. I agree with Miss Rutherford.' He did, too, considerably to his surprise. 'Before we decide to bronchoscope her father, we need to be clear in our minds as to whether he would be fit for surgical intervention. I've heard him wheezing myself, and he has this long history of asthma and bronchitis, you say? What sort of state is his chest in, in your opinion?'

'Until now, I'd thought not too bad. For the past ten years his asthma hasn't troubled him. There's just been his winter bronchitis to watch.'

'You'd class him as an asthmatic bronchitic, then, rather than vice-versa?'

'I would, yes. His wheezing this summer is right out of his usual pattern. But then, sadly, with his heavy smoking and his recurrent bronchitis, it's hardly a surprise, however unwelcome.'

'What we need to do as soon as posible is find out how much his breathlessness is caused by permanent lung damage. What this means, of course, is that we ought to do respiratory function tests before anything else.'

Both his hearers nodded.

'I certainly never believe in carrying out any investigation on a patient merely to satisfy my own curiosity.' Jo brought his gaze abruptly down from the ceiling and directed a quelling glare at Alix. 'It has to be in the patient's own interest. So we'll go ahead and test your father's lung function. Right?'

Dr Lomax looked gloomy. 'Another hurdle. Tomograms *and* respiratory function tests, and then, very likely, the bronchoscopy.' He shook his head. 'He won't like it.'

'Well, I can't arrange for the entire X-ray department from St Mark's to go to Field End for tomograms,' Jo said, his mouth quirking in a manner that Alix found quite fascinating, 'but there's no earthly reason why I shouldn't bring a spirometer with me and do lung function tests next time I play chess with him. So I'll handle that little problem.'

Alix felt relief sweep through her. This fantastic man. She longed to throw her arms round him and hug him on the spot. But it would never do. 'That's tremendously kind of you,' she said, in a cool, senior Sister's voice. 'I'm afraid he won't be exactly easy about it, even then, but it certainly should help matters along in the right direction.'

'Leave it to me.' Jo, in his turn, adopted a distant and strictly professional tone. He'd been nettled by her apparently dismissive response to what had been an extraordinarily generous offer on his part. 'Help matters along in the right direction,' indeed. Thank you very much!

'Then, after that,' Alix persisted, 'if you do think he'd stand surgery, you'd go ahead and bronchoscope him?'

'That's right. And do a biopsy at the same time, probably. And then, if we had to, operate.'

'And pray you can get it all away, if it turns out to be what we have to expect.'

'No need to run ahead of the facts, Alix.' Dr Lomax was soothing.

'I'm thinking about what I'm going to say to him. At some stage I've got to prepare him for admission to St Mark's for the bronchoscopy and the biopsy, very likely to be followed by surgery. He won't like it—how could he? But if I get him to St Mark's for tomograms, and he imagines that's going to be the end of it, and it isn't, he'll say I've deceived him. He'd be right, too.'

'Tell him the truth, would be my advice,' Jo was calm. 'That is, that the investigations are needed to decide what the next step should be. No deception there. After he's had the investigations, then we come to the point where he has to take another decision about surgery. I don't think it's deceitful to leave that decision alone until it has to be made.

After all, he may turn out not to be fit for surgery—in that case why should he be worried over the possibility? You don't have to be standing there wringing your hands warning him we're probably going to have to open up his chest.'

Alix felt well and truly snubbed—yet, at the same moment, amazingly reassured. She bit her lip.

'One step at a time, my dear.' Dr Lomax at his most avuncular.

Jo smiled at her suddenly, a warm and endearing grin that transformed his face—and Alix's world. 'It may sound dull,' he told her, 'but it usually works. And the next step is for me to do his lung function. So leave it to me.'

CHAPTER FOUR

At Long Barn with Jo

THE afternoon saw the first performance of Zoe's play. By the time her own entrance came, Alix was exhausted. Somehow, though, she pulled out all remaining stops, and, Zoe informed her afterwards, went through her few minutes on stage as though inspired.

The audience applauded with frenzy, the cast gathered, and then came the bouquets. First great florists' arrangements for the leading players, and then smaller presentations to their dear ones from the loving families disposed on the lawn in the audience. Finally, to her amazement, the child who had the duty of presenting the flowers came up to Alix with a sheaf of red roses. 'Congratulations and love, Dad,' the accompanying card read. Her eyes misted. One of Daniel's unexpected and touching gestures, coming, as they invariably did, out of the blue. It wasn't even as if he liked her acting in Zoe's plays, either. He hated it, though he'd never tried to stop her. He had agonised memories, Zoe had explained to her, of his brief and unsuccessful marriage. Acting, the theatre, the cinema—none of them were for him, ever again.

She buried her face in the roses, and their scent surrounded her. Their petals, crisp and fresh, brushed her lips, and she found she was vowing that somehow she would see her father through this illness and out

the other side. Everything else in her life must take
second place.

She'd explained this to Woody that morning. 'Thank
you for alerting Dr Lomax. Dad would just have
gone on saying nothing until his book was finished,
I'm sure.'

'I was so worried, Alix. I didn't know what to do. I
didn't like going behind his back, but Sam and I
talked about it, and we decided I either had to write
to you or tell Dr Lomax. So I told him, because it
seemed quicker.'

'I shall have to stay at home now. Not go back to
the Central.' Alix was abrupt. Her mind was made
up, but even so she hated to hear her voice actually
coming out with her decision. This was it. She was
committed now.

Woody failed utterly to grasp the enormous
importance of this dramatic step. 'It would be nice to
have you here for a bit, anyway,' she said comfortably.
'And you could do with a bit of sea air and feeding
up, if you ask me. Been working too hard for months,
you must have been. Have a bit of a rest at home,
dearie, get your father into hospital and home again
for a bit of convalescence, and then you can go back
off to your London life.'

Put like that, it sounded simple.

'I shall get a job down here.' This was something
else she had planned in the early hours of the past
two mornings.

'Oh, surely you don't need to do that. Whatever
for? It isn't as if you need the money, so why not
have a bit of a rest?'

Alix shook her head, more vehemently than was
reasonable. 'I couldn't possibly stay at home doing
nothing. I just need to be around to see that Dad
gets investigated and has his treatment, that's
all.' Clearly Woody had no understanding of the

seriousness of her father's illness. In that case there
was no need to warn her. No point in having two
depressed and worried people at Field End, as well
as a sick Daniel Rutherford.

Her real reasons for deciding to look for a local
job were mixed. Giving up her new post at the
Central was bad enough. To leave nursing altogether,
while her father deteriorated and she watched him go
downhill, would be unbearable. She'd find a job and
live at home. This would mean she was on hand to
arrange her father's treatment and see he followed it;
she'd be with him until the end, if the end had to
come, or until he was fit again, if somehow they
could pull this off. At the same time, though, she'd
go on nursing, go on with her own life. Not sit about
expecting the worst. 'I shall go and see them at St
Mark's,' she told Woody. 'See what posts are coming
up there.'

Woody sniffed. 'No good me trying to talk you out
of it,' she said. 'Any more than I could stop your
father, if he was set on something. But I think you
push yourself too hard, just the same.'

'Not to worry, Woody.' Alix went off to telephone
St Mark's, where the office at once made an
appointment for her to see the Principal Nursing
Officer, Mrs Carlisle.

Promptly at ten-thirty the next morning Alix
presented herself. Jo Standish would hardly have
recognised the trim, well-groomed girl, wearing a suit
in a soft heathery tweed, low-heeled walking shoes,
and subdued make-up.

She was received with open arms. A sister from the
Central who lived locally and wanted to work at St
Mark's. A gift from the gods. Alix said nothing about
Daniel's illness, mentioning only that her home was
in the countryside outside Halchester, and she felt it
was time to return here from London, now that she

was fully trained and had been offered a departmental Sister's post.

'I have to make up my mind now,' she told Mrs Carlisle. 'Because my next appointment at the Central would be Sister General Theatres. Once I accepted it, I'd have to put the whole of myself into it. I know myself, and I know the general theatres. Once I took it on, I'd think of nothing else.' If only she could. A dream of happiness, it seemed now. Here she was, busily throwing her life's ambition down the drain. However, no one at St Mark's must ever be allowed to suspect this. As far as they were concerned, St Mark's was where she wanted to be.

'I think I have a post more or less tailor-made for you,' Mrs Carlisle informed her, thanking her stars that at the moment this outstanding candidate presented herself, she had the right post ready and waiting. 'We are opening a day surgery centre on the first of the month—the idea is to cut down on our waiting lists, and also avoid the usual disruption of patients' lives, by taking suitable cases in for surgery at eight in the morning and returning them home the same evening. I haven't anyone suitable on the staff to act as Sister-in-Charge, and though we advertized, we didn't appoint anyone—none of the candidates who put in for the post were up to it, we felt. If you'd like it, the post could be yours—subject, of course, to my taking up your references, but I'm sure that will present no problem.'

'It sounds just the sort of post I'd like,' Alix said. It was, too. If she couldn't be at the Central, this post would be the next best thing. It was much better than anything she'd been hoping for, far more interesting, and offering her the chance not only to be in at the opening of a new unit, but to be in charge of it.

She went straight home, and rang Miss Frobisher at the Central.

Now she'd wrenched her life into new lines, and all she had to do was live it. There was unlimited time ahead of her to watch over her father, see that he was properly investigated and that he followed whatever treatment was prescribed. As a start, she rang St Mark's again, and made an appointment early the following week for his tomograms. And now it was lunch time. Her father appeared from his writing room, looking pale and drawn, and wheezing badly. She thanked him for the roses.

He was touched by her delight. More than a little guilty, too. Zoe had told him he ought to attend at least one of the performances, but he'd refused. 'Impossible. Can't be done. Middle of my book. No time.' Now he pushed Woody's roast lamb and redcurrant jelly uneasily round his plate, and tried to make himself say he'd be there, watching Alix at the final performance. But the words refused to come.

No, he decided as usual, the book was what counted. Even more so, in fact, if these bloody doctors were right, and he was on the brink of serious illness. Before he gave in to them, he had to finish this book. This particular one was going to be a landmark in his writing career, he was sure of it, and he'd continue to put it first until it was finished. Before his health. Before Alix's pleasure.

A bit hard, that. He ate a mouthful of lamb, and reached a compromise. 'Tell you what. I won't come to the performance—can't spare the time—but I'll collect you afterwards and we'll go out to dinner. Long Barn, say.'

He'd taken Alix to Long Barn only once before, for her twenty-first birthday. 'Dad, how super! I'd love that.' She almost added, 'are you sure you can spare the time?', but swallowed the enquiry as soon as it surfaced. To hand him an opportunity to back out would be plain silly.

'When will you be through?'

'The curtain comes down at six-thirty, but—'

'I'll pick you up at six-forty-five, then. We can have a drink, and I'll book a table for seven-thirty.'

Alix knew better than to protest at the early hour. Her father had always been like this. If he did occasionally agree to any sort of evening celebration, whether at home or, even more infrequently, at a restaurant, invariably he wanted to get it out of the way as soon as possible, so that he could return to his book for a few more hours before bed.

'Don't stand any nonsense from Zoe,' he was saying. 'Tell her I expect you to be punctual. Otherwise she'll try and keep you there clearing up for hours. And I'm not settling for supper with her and Humphrey, either, so don't let her talk you into anything like that.'

'I won't. There is just one thing, though. I shan't have time, if you pick me up at a quarter to seven, to wash and dry my hair. Would you mind if I come to Long Barn with it in purple spikes? Or would you be embarrassed?'

Daniel hardly listened. 'Shouldn't have thought so. But if you're bothered about people noticing, you could wear a scarf or something, couldn't you?'

Great. Dinner at Long Barn, the most prestigious rendezvous for miles around, and she had to appear in her ancient purple cords, her head swathed in any old scarf.

Alone in the dressing room—the cast were still standing around in the conservatory swilling Pimms and yelling their heads off—Alix wondered as she removed her make-up what Zoe would unearth in the way of a scarf for her. For far from trying to make Alix and Daniel stay to help with the clearing up,

Zoe had backed the Long Barn excursion with enthusiasm. 'Marvellous,' she said. 'Daniel is for once going to do his duty and take you to a really nice restaurant. I'll look you out a super evening scarf, darling.'

Would she remember, though, in all the excitement?

She remembered. As Alix fastened the black silk shirt she'd decided to wear with her purple trousers, to replace Tessa's magenta sweater and the leather chain-bedecked jacket, now returned to their owner, Zoe zoomed in waving a long Indian silk scarf in mauve and silver. 'Here you are, darling, this should do. Mind you, I must say your hair looks very nice as it is. Does something for you. Why don't you simply brush it out a bit, so that it's less spiky?' Blonde head on one side, she considered. 'No, I suppose Daniel would never stand for it,' she said regretfully. 'Pity. You'd better wear the scarf. Daniel and purple hair— no, I'm afraid not.' She held out the scarf. 'Here you are, and I've brought you these. They ought to suit you.' She offered her amethyst pendant, together with the amethyst drop ear-rings she wore with it.

Alix was awed. 'Gosh, are you sure? They'd be heaven, but don't you want them yourself?'

'Not tonight, Josephine. Put them on and let's see. Lovely. I'm not sure the scarf isn't a good idea, after all. Suddenly you look a very sophisticated lady. Daniel ought to be proud of you. And take this jacket, too, in case it's cold later.' The jacket was a drift of purple mohair, light as a cloud, unmistakably bought around South Molton Street and probably costing a small fortune. 'Off you go, and enjoy yourself. You've been a tremendous help—I couldn't have done without you. Sorry you haven't time for some Pimms, but better not keep Daniel waiting.'

'Thanks for the scarf and all the jewellery and everything.' Checking herself swiftly in the big mirrors,

Alix was startled to discover that just as Zoe had
said, she looked great. Chic. Almost beautiful?

In the drive, her father was standing by the Porsche
talking to the Lomaxes and Jo Standish. Oops. Had
they been in the audience? The Lomaxes and Jo
Standish?

They had. Dr Lomax—big and rubicond in hairy
off-duty tweed, in contrast to Jo, in dark pinstripe and
a Central tie—congratulated Alix on her performance.
'That walk of yours,' he chuckled. 'Wouldn't have
believed you had it in you if I hadn't seen it with my
own eyes. Hear Daniel's taking you to Long Barn—
you deserve it.'

Her father allowed her no opportunity to reply.
'Come on, then.' He urged her towards the car. 'No
need to hang about for ever. 'Bye, Monica, Basil.
Nice seeing you both. In you get, Alix. And Jo—
forgot to tell you, dear, we're giving Jo a lift to Long
Barn.'

'Oh, are we? Er—how nice. I'll sit in the back,
then.' Alix plonked herself down on the back seat
before there could be any argument about it, and
then wondered why she had ever imagined there
might be. Both men established themselves in the
two front seats as if they took it completely for
granted, rather as if, she felt, she was an intruding
schoolchild being given a lift, her existence barely
registering.

From the conversation drifting back from the front
of the car, it seemed that Jo Standish lived at Long
Barn. Alix often heard that Mrs Armitage, the owner
and manager, did occasionally let rooms, mainly to
staff from St Mark's, where her son-in-law worked.

'I have a sitting-room, and a small bedroom, with a
bathroom between,' Jo was telling her father. 'And I
either have my meals there or at the hospital. It saves
time and trouble, and it's not all that extravagant,

when you consider the expenses I don't have as a result.'

'Seems a thoroughly sensible plan to me. Presumably you'll be eating there this evening, eh? Why not join Alix and me? We're going to push the boat out a bit—we very rarely have a meal out together, so when we do it's a celebration—but I daresay you won't mind that.'

'Far from it. Sounds great. I'd be glad to join you both, if I may.'

So he did remember she was there in the back of the car. That was something.

They parked the car and went into the great entrance hall at Long Barn, which rose to the full height of the massive timbered roof. Justin Armitage, the architect who'd won numerous awards in the fifties and sixties, had converted the barn for his own family, and after his early death his widow had made it the best restaurant for miles around. Tonight, Saturday, it was packed. The bar was jammed, and the small lounge adjoining the restaurant bursting at the seams. There were even groups having their drinks on the wide landing halfway up the wide oak staircase.

'I've booked a table for seven-thirty,' Daniel said. 'Perhaps we could have our drinks out here too—far too much of a mob through there in the bar, don't you think?'

'Far too much,' Jo agreed. 'Why not come up to my sitting-room? It'll be comparatively peaceful, and they'll bring the drinks up to us.' Suddenly, he knew he had somehow to get this amazing girl into his own sitting-room. He wanted her there with a force that staggered him.

'How very kind,' Daniel said, unsuspecting.

Jo led the way up the impressive staircase and along a corridor, and opened his sitting-room door with inexplicable—and well-concealed—triumph. Here she was, this fabulous, unnerving girl, in his own personal territory. What he was going to do with her now he'd got her there he hadn't the faintest idea. He knew all right what he'd like to do, of course. There was only one thing *to* do with a girl with a body like Alix Rutherford, but as that was not on, with her father escorting her, he couldn't understand why he should have so much inner certainty that getting her here was such a satisfying achievement. No doubt, though, that it was.

He busied himself, while his thoughts whirled maddeningly, in fussing away like a good host with the big tweed-covered chairs round the low coffee table, settling Alix into one as if she were frail expensive porcelain liable to shatter—which was not at all how he thought of her. Before she sat down, she slipped the mohair jacket she was wearing off her shoulders, and he took it from her as if he were undressing her, his fingers resting lightly for a brief moment on her slim shoulders. Urgent desire possessed him. Under the mohair she was wearing a thin silk shirt, and the amazing trousers she'd worn for the play, that left nothing to the imagination. Not that this mattered, one way or the other. Jo's imagination was working flat out, with one objective only. An objective he knew to be a waste of time. Inappropriate. Mistaken. Unthinkable.

Not unthinkable. No. Not by any means.

Bemused, his eyes riveted, he heard his voice enquiring about drinks, saw his hand gesturing towards the telephone squatting alongside the *BMJ* and *Lancet* on the coffee table.

'Champagne cocktails. On me. My party,' Daniel said.

Jo picked up the telephone. 'Three champagne cocktails in my upstairs sitting-room.'

They arrived with astonishing speed, Alix considered, remembering the Saturday night crowd jostling downstairs and besieging the bar. Presumably Jo Standish had Long Barn wrapped up and jumping at his lightest word.

Her father, no slouch himself when he did decide to do some entertaining, went into an instant huddle with the pretty Austrian waitress over the table he'd booked, to seat three instead of two, and ordered champagne with the meal.

While he was preoccupied with this Alix leant forward urgently, her eyes looking straight into Jo's. 'Do you think—it does seem a pity when we're supposed to be having a celebration, and he's enjoying himself for once away from his book, but do you think we ought to say something about the tomograms? And then sort of have a go at him about the other investigations?'

Jo looked startled. What he'd expected when Alix had leant forward like that he didn't know. Certainly not an assignation, he wasn't quite out of his mind yet, though not far off. But it was an undoubted shock to find she was planning to turn the evening into a medical consultation.

'I agree it would be a shame to spoil a rare evening out for him. Let him relax and enjoy himself, I'd say. Anyway,' he added, to his own surprise as much as Alix's, 'you're entitled to an evening out and a bit of relaxation, too. You must be worn out—I saw you rushing about all afternoon, backwards and forwards from the stage to the house, non-stop. You must be exhausted. I prescribe an evening off all round, to go with the champagne your father's ordering.'

He'd been watching her. All afternoon.

Daniel sat down and raised his glass. 'Cheers,' he said addressing Jo rather than his daughter.

Jo raised his glass in return, but his eyes went to Alix, and he said, 'Congratulations on your performance.'

She was taken aback. 'Th-thank you.'

Her father's eyes had followed the exchange. 'All right, was she?' he enquired.

'Outstanding, in my opinion.'

'H'mph.' Daniel was divided between pleasure and worry. He liked Alix to do well, naturally, but he didn't want her to follow in her mother's footsteps. Damned acting. He would rather she was good at anything else. He scrutinised her dubiously, and something about her appearance dawned on him for the first time. 'What are you wearing that scarf round your head for? Look as if you're ready to turn out a room. Must be hot, too. No wonder you're a bit red in the face.'

Alix wanted to throttle him. However, one thing she wouldn't do was have a row with her father in front of Jo Standish of all people, so she curbed her rage and said mildly, 'I did explain, Dad, that I wouldn't have time to wash the colour out of my hair, and it was you who said to wear a scarf.' Ready to turn out a room, indeed!

'Oh, did I? Well, up here it would hardly matter if your hair were all colours of the rainbow, would it? Jo won't mind, I'm sure, and there's no one else to notice. You might as well cool down a bit, if you ask me.'

Red-faced and sweating like a pig, she must be, and her face shining like a beacon.

Jo didn't know where he stood—let alone where he wanted to stand—with this incredible girl, but he couldn't get away from the fact that everything about her seemed to matter extraordinarily. He experienced in his own bones her rage with her father, and now he rushed to her assistance. 'That scarf suits you, I'd say, but your hair was terrific in the play. I'm all for having another sight of it.'

Alix looked immensely relieved, and for the first time it occurred to Jo that she might not be nearly as confident as he'd imagined, and certainly her father did nothing to bolster her ego. All right, so he was a best-selling author, and Jo liked and respected him, but as a parent he seemed to verge on the negligent. A sudden longing, not any longer to make urgent, demanding love to this lovely incredible girl but instead to enfold her safely for ever in loving, protective, caring arms swept through Jo.

He must be out of his mind.

Alix wasn't looking for any tender loving care from a middle-aged consultant like himself. He should be so lucky. Ha!

She was unwinding the long Indian scarf somewhat dubiously, and then ruffling up her purple hair. She squinted uncertainly at herself in the tiny mirror of her compact, her eyes bothered.

'My bathroom's through there, if you want to tidy up.' Jo jerked his head. 'Not that you need to. You look perfectly all right.' Perfectly all right. What an asinine thing to say.

'Oh, thank you. I would like to.' Alix walked across the room to the door in the far wall, away from the coffee table and the easy chairs, past what was obviously Jo's desk and a long low bookshelf, never guessing that his eyes remained glued hopefully to her small purple behind, wanting it to behave as it had done when she walked across the stage. No joy. He sighed.

In the bathroom, Alix repaired her make-up, twitched at her hair, and decided that in fact, whatever her father might think, she looked really quite nice. Zoe's ear drops seemed to suit her. So, in a weird way, did the purple hair. She must stop feeling like a silly schoolgirl, out with the grown-ups for a treat, and get herself back into the confident, couldn't-care-less role she'd successfully adopted in the play. Her father had brought her here for a celebration, and she was going to enjoy herself, however much cold water her infuriating parent chose to drown her in. Tomorrow she had to face up to a great deal that she hated to think about. Tomorrow she had to do something about her father's future and her own. Tonight she was going to enjoy champagne and Long Barn food. Even, perhaps, Jo Standish's company. This evening he had transformed himself into a different personality.

She shook her purple hair defiantly and sailed back into the sitting-room, and, shortly, down the great oak staircase to the restaurant, across the crowded room to their table. Jo followed her all the way, his eyes locked on to her delightful rear view behaving in exactly the way he had longed for it to behave.

They settled down at their table and Daniel ordered, champagne was poured, smoked trout arrived, and they began to eat. Jo, who had been so nice and approachable only a few minutes earlier, now wore a forbidding expression and said hardly anything.

What had got into him? Had she done something to annoy him?

She knew at once what it must be. The wiggle. Obviously it had put him right off, just when he'd seemed to be changing, becoming so approachable. Why on earth had she done it?

Well, to assert herself, of course. Because she was feeling one down, and she'd decided to put a stop to that. OK, so she'd changed everything, if that was what she wanted, she'd done it.

She drank uneasily—and was cured. To hell with men and their moods. She'd walk about wherever she chose in whatever way it occurred to her to walk. Who was Jo Standish anyway? What right had he to disapprove of anything she did? She'd show him. She'd show the world.

What she would have shown them she never found out, because at this moment her father—the champagne going a little to his head, too—began doing something she'd never known him to do before. He opened up and began telling them about his current book.

'It's a new departure, you see.'

Alix had known nothing of this. Every year he wrote a spy thriller, set in Europe during World War Two. These were the books he'd made his name writing—it had been the first of these that had brought him the film option, and then the film, during which he'd gone to Hollywood to work on the script and met her mother. Since then he'd written more than fifteen or sixteen of them, not all of them filmed, but all of them televised. The public loved them.

'It's still a spy story,' he said, 'but set a good deal further back. In Plantagenet times.'

Alex digested this. He was a historian, of course, and this was his favourite period. He knew it inside out. 'But—but what will your publisher think?'

'There's the nub of it. I don't know. I want to make sure it's working, you see, before I commit myself. If it's no good, I shall simply put it away in a drawer, and get back to my usual line.'

'Do you think it is working? As far as you've got?' The question came from Jo.

Daniel's eyes sparkled in a way, Alix suddenly

realised, they never did for people. Only for books.
'Oh yes, it's working like mad, as far as I'm
concerned.'

'How far along are you?' Jo asked.

'Nearly at the end of the first draft. When I
complete it I shall read it right through at a sitting,
and then I'll probably know. If it seems all right,
I'll let Celia—my editor—see it, and get her
reaction.'

'It sounds extraordinarily like trying to pass the
Fellowship. You must be worried.'

'I'm worried all right—when I stop to think about
it. Most of the time, though, I don't. I simply get
on with writing it.'

'Yes, I can understand that.' Jo spoke slowly,
and his dark eyes flashed some message to Alix—
but she was so startled at being on the receiving
end of any communication from him that she
entirely failed to read whatever it was he'd sent
her.

'So you see I can't let anything, anything at all,
come between me and it at present. My health will
have to wait.' Her father stared challengingly across
the table.

'But Dad—' Alix began.

Jo shook his head fractionally, and interrupted
her. 'When you say you're nearing the end of the
first draft, what precisely do you mean?'

So that's what he'd been indicating by that first
glance, Alix decided. Don't raise the questions of
his treatment.

Daniel shrugged. 'I wish I knew. But I don't. It
depends how it goes. Could be a couple of weeks,
could be more like a couple of months.'

'I see,' was all Jo said, though his eyes sent
another message to Alix, and this time she

recognised it for what it was. A warning. Don't argue with him.

All right, she wouldn't. He could handle it. Surprising herself, Alix relaxed into the inner certainty that seemed to take possession of her when Jo was around. Security was where Jo was. He knew how to handle any problem. All she had to do was follow his lead.

Follow his lead? What could she be thinking of? What she ought to be concentrating on was what her father was saying. That was where her attention should be, not wrapped up in Jo Standish and how she felt about him.

Her father seemed to be embarking on the story of his book. 'The central character, the spy, is a poet. Based on Chaucer, really—that's how the idea came to me. And like all the best ideas I couldn't get away from it. It wouldn't leave me alone. I'd already drafted the next wartime thriller, but somehow I couldn't get down to it. Chaucer and the fourteenth century kept playing themselves out on top of it. So in the end I gave in.'

'Was Chaucer a spy?' Jo was intrigued.

'He was a diplomat, in the royal service. He may or may not have done some spying on the side. But this character of mine isn't Chaucer any longer. I've built him up now, and he goes his own way.'

'Fascinating.'

Daniel gave a short laugh. 'That's the word. He certainly fascinates me, and I can't leave him alone. Won't.' Again he threw a challenge across the table, and again Jo failed to rise to it.

'Tell me what happens,' he said, apparently no other thought in his head but a desire to know what went on in Daniel's book.

Daniel was pleased, and, his confidence restored, ate the tender fillet steak placed in front of him as blindly as if it had been hamburger and chips, and related the complete plot of his book.

All three of them moved back to the fourteenth century, while steak and salad gave way to blackberry cheesecake, and the pretty Austrian waitress poured the last of their champagne, asking if they would like another bottle.

'Another?' Daniel broke off. 'Finished that, have we? Yes, bring another bottle.'

'But Dad—'

'Not on my account,' Jo began. 'I—'

They were instantly overruled. 'Another bottle,' Daniel repeated.

When it arrived and was poured. Alix put her hand over her glass. Someone had to stay sober to drive the Porsche. It was maddening, though, to hear her father, spotting her gesture, agree that she'd had enough, as if she were a schoolgirl trying out her first drink.

Jo noticed the interchange, and his eyes glinted, but he said nothing, and Daniel resumed his account of Plantagenet days. He and Jo demolished the champagne, coffee came, and still her father talked. Alix had never known anything like it.

Eventually, though, the evening came to an end, and Jo and Alix drifted out to the great hall together while Daniel was settling the bill.

'He's really enjoyed himself,' Alix said.

'Done him good. Would have been useless, not to mention have deprived him of a great deal of pleasure, to have tried to make him drop this book and accept treatment immediately. Waste of time. Don't believe in useless arguments with patients who aren't going to listen. Better to save your energies for a more propitious occasion.'

Alix spoke abruptly. 'I shall stay here at home,

you know, and see him through. I shan't be taking up my post at the Central.'

Jo looked startled out of his wits, and then—surely she must be imagining it? Oh, surely—delighted. His eyes flooded with a warmth she'd never seen in them before, and he grinned like a carefree boy.

Her father joined them. That explained it, of course. He'd been looking across at Daniel, not thinking about her at all. The disappointment was acute. And ridiculous, she told herself angrily.

CHAPTER FIVE

Alix and Daniel

On Sundays, Woody didn't come to Field End, and Alix, throughout her childhood, had spent the day at Zoe's. This had ensured that she was fed and supervised, while allowing Daniel to write in peace. As she'd grown older, Alix had continued to spend Sunday with Zoe. To do so had become traditional.

She would be expected there this Sunday. The problem was she hadn't yet spoken to her father—not about his treatment, not about her own plan to remain at Field End, not about the post at St Mark's. Last night she'd even told Jo Standish she was staying at home with Daniel, and today it would be almost impossible to avoid telling Zoe—she could hardly spend the day with her and maintain the pretence she'd be leaving to return to the Central at the end of the week. By this evening, three people would know of her plans. Only Daniel himself would be left in ignorance. It wouldn't do.

Should she tackle him before she left for Zoe's? To interrupt him at work in the morning was to break all the rules. On the other hand, this was important.

Perhaps if he hadn't been so forthcoming the previous evening about his book she might have gone over to the writing room. But after last night she couldn't. On the way home, he'd gone broody and silent, a mood she was used to. For the first time, though, she'd recognised it for what it was. He'd been talking about his book, and now he'd gone right back into it. He'd said good night briefly, and gone back into his writing room. She wouldn't be surprised to learn that he'd written until the small hours. Now he might at last be sleeping, or he might be back at his typewriter.

She couldn't burst in and start talking about his health, his treatment, and her own decision not to return to the Central until he'd been investigated. Jo had been right last night. That had not been the moment, and first thing this morning was not the moment either. But, on the other hand, she couldn't drift along indefinitely, making her own plans round him, informing everyone else—even Woody knew— and not saying a word to him.

Today she had to tell him.

Well, what the hell. Sunday at Zoe's was not an edict from on high. She'd stay at home, and catch her father when he surfaced, which he'd be bound to do at some stage, even if it wasn't until a mid-afternoon lunch.

She picked up the telephone, rang Zoe, and told her she wouldn't be over to lunch, she was having a quiet day at home. 'Could I return the pendant and the ear-rings some time tomorrow? Would that be all right? They were super—thanks so much for lending them to me.'

'Of course, darling. Or hang on to them until the end of your holiday—they suited you, so why not wear them while you're down here?'

Alix felt a heel. Zoe was so kind, and here she was, practically lying to her, pretending she'd be going back to the Central at the end of the week. She set her chin. It couldn't be helped. Zoe might be sweet and kind, but Daniel came first. 'Thanks terribly,' she said. 'Angelic of you. I certainly felt marvellous wearing them—you're quite right, they do something for me.'

'Did you have a good evening?'

'Champagne until it was practically coming out of our ears.'

'Oh, I *am* so glad. Daniel owes you an evening like that. He doesn't do enough.'

Alix changed the subject to the play, saying how successful it had been. Zoe was safely diverted, and discussed the ins and outs of the casting, the timing, and what she was planning for next year's season. 'You're sure you won't pop over for lunch?' she asked finally. 'There's so much to talk about.'

'Not today, thanks. I've been here nearly a week, and I've hardly seen Dad, apart from last night.'

And that was the truth, she thought as she put the telephone down. But today she was going to see him and have it out with him, if she had to hang around all day.

She did some chores around the house, renewing the flowers—a few late roses for her bedroom, and a great bowl of tawny chrysanthemums for the old oak chest in the living-room—put a load of washing through the machine in the utility room, and then settled down with the Sunday papers on the garden terrace in the autumn sun. From here she could keep an eye on Daniel—she'd be able to spot him as soon as he came down from the writing room. The little terrace had been one of the improvements made when the garage and the writing room were built, it was tucked in at the side of the house, sheltered from the north by the utility room and the garage porch, into which the stairs from the writing room led.

He appeared about one-thirty, waved to her, and came out on to the terrace, looking—and sounding—

surprised. 'Never occurred to me you'd be here—
thought you'd be going to your aunt's, as usual.'

'I rang and put her off. Felt like a day at home —
I've hardly been here since I arrived.'

'True enough. Has she been working you too
hard? She gets so enthusiastic about those plays of
hers, never lets up.'

'It was quite fun,' Alix said, 'but enough is
enough.'

'I'll get you a drink—that's what I've come down
for, so you might as well join me.'

'Thanks, Dad, I'd like that.'

'Short or long?'

'After all that super champagne last night, I think
I'll stick to orange juice this morning.'

'Good idea. May do that myself.' He went off
into the house.

Now for it. She had to have it out with him,
while they drank their orange juice, and before he
disappeared again.

She began badly. 'I'm not going back to the
Central after all.'

That shook him all right. He gaped at her. 'But
why not? You were so pleased about your new
post—you told me so. How can you have decided
suddenly not to go back?' He was shocked, and a
flicker of panic had crept in, too. Surely that
damned play of Zoe's hadn't gone to her head? She
wasn't thinking of throwing up her hospital career
to try and make out as an actress?

He was wrong, of course. But her answer threw
him completely.

'That was before I'd seen you, Dad. You're not
well.'

For God's sake, now what? Silly of him. He'd
been worried about the possibility that she might be
dreaming of the theatre, and overlooked the fact

that she was a fully trained nurse. That was something he'd never taken into account. 'Just my usual cough,' he said evasively.

'More like your usual bronchitis. And in September, not mid-winter.'

'Yes, well, I know. Dreadful weather, that's what's done it, I dare say. Cold, damp summer. Might as well have been winter. Once I've got this book out of the way I'll go to Switzerland, have a good holiday and some decent mountain air. That always clears me up. Did the trick as a child, and it'll do it again now. Soon put me right.'

'No, it won't, Dad. It's no use. I haven't worked in hospital for over five years without being able to tell whether people are well or ill, you know. You're ill. I only have to look at you to know. Anyway, I've seen Dr Lomax, and he agrees with me. So don't try kidding me.'

Her father looked as though the terrace had risen up from the ground and hurled itself at him.

'I understand why you can't drop your book at this stage,' Alix went on, 'but I'm not leaving here until you're sorted out. And that's that. I've told them at the Central, and I've been to see them at St Mark's. They've offered me a post there. So that's it. I'll be sticking around here, at least until your chest is back to normal.' Back to normal, indeed. What a hope.

Daniel showed no gratitude. More irritation. 'I'm no company for anyone when I'm finishing a book,' he pointed out. 'And I don't want people around, either. Not even you. No one. Sorry, I don't mean that quite the way it sounds.' Even he, apparently, noticed something badly wrong with his response. 'But I don't want you hanging around here out of some misplaced sense of duty, because you've taken it into your head I'm your ailing decrepit Dad, and you have to throw up your career in London to come home and look after me.'

'I'm not giving up any career to look after you,' Alix told him, thinking how fortunate it was that she had applied to St Mark's for a post. 'I'm taking a different job, that's all. A very interesting one, I may say. I'm not proposing to hang around smoothing your brow and offering nourishing drinks of beef tea or barley water. I don't want to look after you. All I want is for you to look after yourself for a change. And I shall stick around until you do.'

Daniel looked hunted. 'I'm not used to sharing the house with anyone else. Naturally I'm very fond of you, Alix, you know that.'

Did she? Not really. It certainly didn't sound like it at the moment.

'But I prefer my own company most of the time. Particularly when I'm in the middle of a book. I have to be alone to do my writing. I can't write with anyone else around the place—that's why I had the writing room built.'

It was, was it? To get away from her, his darling daughter. Marvellous. 'Don't panic, Dad,' she said coolly. 'I'll be out at work most of the time. But I'm not going back to London. Not until the problem of your chest is sorted out. If you want to get rid of me, you'll have the investigations Dr Lomax and Jo Standish are advising, and then maybe we'll know where we stand. I'm staying here until you're fit again.' If only she could believe that that was likely.

'There's not the faintest need for you to take up this attitude,' her father said irritably, together with much more to the same effect—and in the same irritated, if not exasperated, manner. Both of them swallowed their orange juice, went into a lunch of cold meat and salad and consumed it, without their argument ceasing. Neither would give in, and in the end they reached stalemate. Alix gave up the struggle and went for a walk, while Daniel went back to his writing.

Shut safely away in his writing room, though, he began to experience emotions that had nothing to do with the fourteenth century.

No one had ever put him first. No one had made a sacrifice for him. His young wife, indeed, had refused to do anything of the sort, in no uncertain terms.

'What, give up my chances here in Hollywood, give up all this, to go back to that poky little cottage to look after you and a screaming toddler? When we can all three stay here, and pay for a nurse without any problems? Thank you, but I'm not wearing that. You go, if you want to, and if you hate it so much here. I'm not coming. You'd better take Alix with you, if you're going, and try looking after her yourself.' She hadn't expected him to do it, he'd known that at the time. It had been no more than a trivial quarrel, in her eyes. But he'd left, and he'd taken Alix with him.

He'd imagined, of course, that she'd come to her senses and follow him. But she had stayed in Hollywood.

But now that little baby, his daughter, was putting him first. For whatever she might say about this new job at St Mark's, she must have wanted to stay at the Central. She'd been so pleased about the post she'd landed there. She told him about it in the car on the way home, he remembered clearly. He hadn't taken it in at the time, he'd been preoccupied with the next chapter, which had suddenly begun playing itself out to him, so that all he'd wanted was to get to the typewriter and capture it. But he had a reliable tape recorder whirring away inside his skull, and it played meticulously over to him, later on that night, and again now, this afternoon, exactly what Alix had said about her new post. She'd really cared about it. Now she'd given it up. Not only given it up, but been along to the local hospital, without him knowing anything at all about it, and organised herself into a quite different job. All for him.

His little daughter had gone. In her place stood an adult. A resolute adult, who loved him. And could stand up to him.

He loved her deeply. How deeply he had never quite understood before. He'd known he was fond of her, naturally. But that there was this deep bond between them he'd been unaware. Unaware, he told himself, ashamed, until Alix had demonstrated it to him.

Much later that night, after he'd put in a good stint on the book, he sat on at his desk and wondered what he was going to do. Could Alix be right? And if she was, what did he owe her, as opposed to what he owed to his writing and his reputation?

That he owed her something was beginning to dawn on him. All very well to decide for himself that what mattered was his book, that only after it was finished would he start thinking about his health, but what about Alix? If she could give up a job she'd longed for simply because she was worried about him, ought he to put the book on one side and have these investigations they were all so keen on?

Was there the slightest chance that early investigation might make a difference to the outcome? They'd all said so, but he hadn't believed them. He'd been assuming that he was finished anyway.

This spot on his lung they were so excited about was going to be the end of him, and that was that. For months he'd been feeling awful, now they'd found the cause, and that was as far as he wanted to go, thank you very much. If he was doomed, so be it. But he'd finish his book before he went.

However, if Alix was right, everything would be different. How was he to know where he stood?

Alix. He'd have to trust her, do as she advised. That would mean giving in and having more X-rays—tomograms or whatever they were called. Give up an afternoon. That would have to be the end of it, though. After that, back to the book and no more interruptions. He nodded, satisfied with the result of his careful assessment, and a little pleased with himself. Pleased with Alix, too. As a daughter, she was quite something.

What he never for an instant suspected was that Alix was far from pleased with him. Cheesed off was more like it.

She walked for a long time that afternoon—along the cliffs, down the steep path to the harbour, and then along the path by the salt marshes. Furious with Daniel—and herself, too—she walked fast and angrily. What the hell had she imagined she was doing, deciding to give up her job and stay here in Halchester? Obviously Daniel didn't want her. She must have been mad to throw up her post at the Central. Impulsively, she'd rushed straight into a decision she need never have taken. Once she had discussed Daniel with Jo and Dr Lomax, all she had needed to do was to leave him in their capable hands. She could have gone back to the Central at the end of the week and begun her new job as planned. So simple. So easy. So infinitely rewarding. But she'd blown it. Announcing dramatically that no one but herself could possibly look after Daniel, she had thrown up her new post, and now here she was. No job at the Central, and Daniel didn't want her at Field End.

Hold it. All right, he didn't want her. He might still need her, though. What if he did have lung cancer? What if these investigations had to be followed immediately by surgery and radiotherapy? She could hardly, whatever he might say, leave his care then to Jo and St Mark's, and his convalescence to Woody, with Dr Lomax looking in several times a week. At that stage she'd have to be at Field End. And that stage might be approaching very fast indeed.

Perhaps she hadn't been so silly, after all. Better to install herself at Field End now, rather than have to come rushing back from the Central at a day's notice.

She shook her head. Whether she'd made the right decision or not, the fact was that the Central was no longer part of her life. She'd handed in her notice, she was staying in Halchester and working at St Mark's. Too late to back out. What she had to do was to make the best of it. In any case, there was no reason why the job shouldn't prove both worthwhile and interesting. No reason why she shouldn't enjoy it. It would be good for her to make new friends and work somewhere different. She'd had six years at the Central. Time she moved on to new challenges. New opportunities.

One of these, she suddenly realised, was coming towards her across the marshes at this minute.

Jo Standish, his hair tousled in the wind like her own, his large form clad this afternoon not in a consultant's formal pinstripe, but in faded cords topped by an Aran sweater and a shabby-looking windcheater.

A signal from fate. Here, Alix Rutherford, is your new life.

Jo's reaction was entirely different.

One of his rare free weekends had been ruined for him. He'd woken this morning with his mind obsessed with the past. With Olivia.

Olivia, the beautiful girl he'd married, her illness—she had one of the lethal forms of leukaemia—already beyond any chance of a cure. All they dared hope for was a remission.

He'd met her first in the wards, when he'd been a fifth-year student. For two long strenuous years, during which he'd qualified and held down two demanding house jobs, he'd fought his overwhelming love for her. And then, against the advice of every friend he possessed and to the displeasure of his seniors and the fury of his chief, Leo Rosenstein, he married her.

He also put down a deposit on a flat he could barely afford, because it was within yards of the hospital, had central heating and enough space for her to be nursed at home. He offered one room free to a staff nurse he knew, provided she promised to be there at night to look after Olivia, and himself took a post—easily obtained, since the hours were unpopular and the job led precisely nowhere—as night casualty officer.

His friends despaired. He was throwing his career down the drain for a girl already dying. In a year or two she'd be gone, and then where would he be? No wife. No career. No future.

They'd been right, of course, and he'd known it. But he had to follow his own path. Love for Olivia fused with the urge for caring that had led him into medicine in the first place, and he was ready and eager to give up everything that had previously mattered in order to devote himself to this tragic girl he adored.

Olivia was loving as well as beautiful, and while she had the strength she adored him, too. In the first few months of their marriage they knew high peaks of rapture and depths of closeness that transcended all else. Too soon, though, it was downhill all the way, and pain took over from ecstasy. Even before her body finally succumbed to the disease that killed her, Jo had to watch love fade away. Exhausted by her illness, Olivia had little to offer, and what she increasingly wanted from Jo was to be cherished and protected, to be wrapped securely in a devotion that would carry her through every low. This Jo gave her, until she died.

He had to pick himself up and start again. He'd done it, but it had been hard going. Determined, unceasing work helped him to survive. He'd cared for his patients, tried to turn his own experience to their benefit. Slowly, against the odds, he rebuilt his abandoned career. Leo Rosenstein, his former chief, had helped him. Jo knew he had been lucky. Leo needn't have bothered. But he was a warm and generous man, as well as a busy surgeon, and he'd put himself out, had asked around and then badgered his colleagues into interviewing Jo whenever they had a suitable vacancy. It had been Leo who found Jo his first registrar's post in thoracic surgery, and Leo, again, who sent him off, away from the Central, to the Birmingham Accident Hospital for his next job.

'Y'need to get away. Too many memories 'ere. No use to you. Counter productive. Clear off to the Midlands and carve y'self a niche away from this place and the past.'

He'd been right. But then Leo usually was. At the Birmingham Accident Hospital Jo started to enjoy his days again. The steady climb back had begun, and was to continue uninterrupted until at last, only a year ago, he'd achieved this consultant post at St Mark's.

Since Olivia had died, though, he'd never loved anyone. The emotion he'd felt for her was no longer in him, it seemed. He'd had easy-going affairs with lovely girls, and he'd enjoyed them, liked them, had fun with them—but that was as far as it went. With Olivia's death, true love had departed for ever, he decided.

Today, out of the blue, Olivia had suddenly returned. This morning, the moment he awoke, the floodgates had opened and memories of her came pouring out.

Restless, uncertain, hating the force of these old emotions that were tearing him apart again, he'd gone off after lunch for a long walk, and now, as he returned across the marshes and the soft west wind ruffled his dark hair and cooled his pounding temples, he began to understand that he might perhaps be ready at last to be healed. It might be time to forget and go forward, free of Olivia.

And now, over the marshes towards him, came another girl. A girl as unlike Olivia as any girl could be.

A girl he didn't want to meet. Not now. Not today.

That extraordinary daughter of Daniel Rutherford's. The purple-haired punk in skin-tight jeans. The jeans were still skin-tight, but today her hair was a perfectly ordinary colour, and her face pale. Her body, though, was as sexy as ever, and he knew exactly what he'd like to do with it.

Unthinkable.

Especially unthinkable after these memories of Olivia. All right, so he might today suspect he was at last ready to move on, to leave Olivia in the past. But goodbye, Olivia, and bless you for ever, my lost love, could never mean 'Come in, Alix, and be my new love.' No way. Alix might have a sexy body and a riveting strut, but anything he felt for her was light years away from true love. She was no sort of girl for him.

Her father was different. He was a friend, and as well, sadly, a patient. Very likely, too, another doomed patient.

With Daniel in his mind, however, thankfully he found it no effort at all, as he came abreast with Alix, to greet her. 'Afternoon, Miss Rutherford. Stretching your legs after lunch like me, eh? How's your father today?'

'Back at his book.' Alix was short. For some inexplicable reason, all she wanted to do was to burst into tears and fling herself on to Jo's broad chest, there to cry her eyes out until she felt better. If she could just hold on to him, she'd be all right.

This was not only ridiculous nonsense, but a blind refusal to face the facts staring her in the face. For here was Jo, on whom for some crazy reason she'd been pinning her hopes for the future, and he turned out to be just another jovial consultant surgeon, ready to chat up any patient's relative with conventional heartiness, his thoughts clearly elsewhere.

'Get him along to the X-ray department as soon as you can, won't you?' he urged her. 'For the tomograms,' he added, to her fury, presumably supposing her to be so thick she wouldn't have known why, unless he spelled it out for her.

'I'll do that,' she agreed politely, hating him more than she would have believed possible even a minute or two earlier.

'Splendid.' He nodded encouragingly, and strode

away from her along the marsh path back towards the harbour.

Without a backward glance, Alix plodded stolidly off in the opposite direction.

CHAPTER SIX

Jo

MONDAY morning at eight o'clock saw Jo on twenty-four-hour call for the accident unit, as he would be until the following Monday. He and the director of the unit covered alternate weeks, during which one or other of them was available as a priority over all other demands. Occasionally on odd days, there might be no night calls and hardly more than a few routine visits to check that there were no problems that the duty team couldn't handle.

Today, though, the ambulance brought in a young driver who'd crashed on the motorway going to work. The anaesthetic registrar saw him in the ambulance and put in an airway, and then, in the shock room nurses cut away his clothing, while the surgical registrar, Martin Fenton, began to examine him. He shook his head. 'I don't like the look of him. Internal bleeding, I'm afraid, as well as the stove-in chest.' In spite of all they had done, the patient's colour remained, ominously, pale mauve.

The anaesthetist was already cutting down into a vein for a drip, while one of the house surgeons was taking blood for cross-matching. The radiographer came in with the portable X-ray machine, and on her heels the senior surgical registrar, summoned by Martin Fenton.

He at once began to examine the patient. 'I agree with you, Martin. Internal bleeding. Almost certainly a ruptured spleen. We must get him into the theatre, stat. If you see to that, I'll get hold of Jo.'

Twenty minutes later they were all in the theatre. The patient had been identified. He was Kevin Neal, and lived in Halchester. His wife was on her way to the hospital.

'How's the patient?' Jo, scrubbed, masked and gowned, half a head taller than any of them—and they weren't short—addressed the anaesthetist.

'I've got the end of the table up as far as it will go.' It was a warning they all understood. 'I'm just about holding him at present, but it'll be touch and go.'

'We'll get in fast and arrest the haemorrhage. How much blood have we? Has he been cross-matched?'

'The lab are working on it. Meanwhile we're ready to collect his own blood for re-use by suction.'

'Good. Hurry the lab up, though. Ready, Sister? Right, we'll go ahead.' He made the first incision, and the complicated emergency surgery on a deteriorating patient—Kevin Neal was on the danger list—was under way.

Four hours later, to their relief, the patient was still alive, and in fact in better condition than when he had first arrived in the theatre.

'Well, that's it. That's about all we can do for now,' Jo said, as he stood back. 'I'll look in and see him in Intensive Care after my meeting with Mrs Carlisle. How's the time going? Wonder if I've a chance of snatching a quick bite first?'

'Mrs Carlisle rang through a few minutes ago,' Theatre Sister told him. 'She asked if you were going to be held up, and said if it would be any help she'd order coffee and sandwiches for you.'

'How very thoughtful. I hope you accepted the offer for me?'

'We did.'

'Many thanks. I'll get down there, then. You can

tell her I'm on my way. Thank you, Sister—everyone.
A more satisfactory session than we expected, I'm
glad to say.'

Ten minutes later, changed and immaculate in a
dark suit tailored in London and a gleaming shirt
with a Central tie, Jo strolled nonchalantly into Mrs
Carlisle's office as if life was one long dawdle.

'Good afternoon, Mr Standish. I hear you missed
out on lunch again—I hope this may bridge the gap.'
She gestured at the tray ready on her desk. 'Coffee?'

'Thank you. This is a real luxury. I didn't expect to
eat until this evening.' He smiled the transforming
smile that had been the talk of the accident unit
when he arrived, and Mrs Carlisle found herself
wishing she'd thought of ordering smoked salmon and
a dry white wine.

'Ham sandwiches,' she said dubiously. 'With
mustard. I hope they'll do.'

'Be great,' Jo said, taking a large bite. 'Cheers,' he
added a moment later, and raised his coffee cup.
'What news do you have for me about the day
surgery centre?'

'Good news, I'm glad to say. I've found you an
exceptionally good Sister-in-Charge, so our worries
about that are over. She'll double as theatre sister, so
with Staff Nurse Proctor as her second-in-command,
you should be well looked after.'

'Splendid. Who is this paragon, and where did you
find her?'

'I can't claim any credit there, I'm afraid. She
found herself. She lives locally, but she comes from
your own hospital, the Central. You may already
know her—Alix Rutherford.'

Jo nearly choked on his ham sandwich.

Mrs Carlisle, though, her eyes searching Alix's
curriculum vitae, failed to notice, and went confidently
on. 'She's Central trained, and has been a junior

Sister in the theatres for the past eighteen months. If she'd stayed they would have made her Sister General Theatres. But there's some sort of family problem, and she wants to live at home. I had a long talk with Miss Frobisher at the Central, and they spoke most highly of her. Said we were lucky to get her, in fact, and they didn't want to lose her. So it seems ideal from our point of view, if not from the Central's.'

'Certainly sounds like it.' Jo had to agree, but the words came out so negatively that Mrs Carlisle was alerted, and shot him a quick probing glance. What could be wrong? At once, though, she recollected the long hours of surgery on a dangerously ill patient, who might so easily have died on the table, a surgeon's nightmare. He was tired out, that was all. She'd let him get his sandwiches down, while she handed out the details he needed before the opening of the centre. So she rattled cheerfully on about junior staff, rotas, the four-day week that would require only a single team to work it, and the essential liaison with the transport office.

One side of Jo's mind kept track of what she was saying and noted it, even volunteering a few appropriate comments. But he was in turmoil.

He couldn't have that purple-haired sex-pot running the new centre, meet her daily to discuss the lists, have coffee in her office—the way he was having it now with Mrs Carlisle—have her assisting him in the theatre. He was damned if he'd stand for any such arrangement.

So what was he going to say to Mrs Carlisle?

Nothing. There was nothing he could say. He could hardly advance, as a reason for turning down the candidate she was so delighted to have found for him, the fact that the girl had spiky purple hair and waggled her bottom, and he'd been half hoping—

much against his better judgement—to have a rip-roaring affair with her.

Anyway, why the hell shouldn't he be able to work with her? Under a theatre turban, it could hardly be of the least consequence what colour her hair was, while he would defy even Alix Rutherford to waggle her neat little bottom at him when she was bunched up in a theatre gown. No, exactly as Mrs Carlisle had pointed out, she was Central-trained and they were lucky to get her. He'd have to put a good face on it.

It would be hell. He'd have her around all day. Depend on her for the proper running of the centre—and keep his hands off her sexy body.

He frowned hideously.

A startled eye assessed him. 'Is there anything wrong, Mr Standish?'

He pulled himself together. 'Nothing whatever.' He braced his broad shoulders, and stretched in his chair. 'Very comfortable here, and I don't feel much inclined to move on. But it's what I must do.' He frowned again, deliberately this time, and levered himself out of his chair with a sigh. 'The coffee and sandwiches were life-saving,' he said. 'Many thanks indeed.' He nodded, and made for Intensive Care.

Before going in, though, he paused, staring out of the window on the landing by the lifts, oblivious of the bustle around him, looking out across the car-park, but seeing only a slight girl with spikes of gleaming purple hair and a body he ached to possess.

It simply wasn't on. There was nóthing he could do about her. There never had been, and now there was less chance than ever that he'd be able to make love to Alix Rutherford, with her sexy body and her impossible ways. Instead he had to run the new centre in partnership with her, of all people, when she represented everything he most detested in women. Everything that was the opposite of Olivia—

though he had to admit that his feelings for her were in their entirely different way quite as unmanageable.

In the case of Olivia, he could see it now, he'd fallen in love partly because he yearned to share her pain. Well, he had done so, and it was over, and he was no longer the same eager, over-confident young house surgeon who had wanted somehow to put everything right for her, or at least to make up to her for all she'd never have. He'd failed, as he'd been bound to, and as they had all warned him he would. It had been inevitable.

Olivia was ten years into the past, and less, now, the wife he'd once had, more a beloved child who'd died. Yet somewhere in him still survived a tender loving boy, who had offered everything, and lost.

Since then, though, he knew he'd never looked in the same way at any girl. He'd had girls in his life, on and off, of course. He hadn't shed all the natural urges because Olivia had gone. He'd lusted after girls, and he'd felt—often—mildly affectionate towards them. But love? Never. Not since Olivia.

Now he wanted Alix. He would have liked to pay back, on Alix's strong and maddeningly seductive frame, the thwarted urges of his sad and unsatisfactory marriage. He wanted to take it all out on Alix. He wanted her so much that merely setting eyes on her sent him, he remembered with a twist of angry lips, into what amounted to a frenzy. Yet at the same moment he almost hated her. For being alive when Olivia was gone. For being strong and fit and standing on her own two feet.

He would have liked to be free to grab Alix, hurl her against the nearest wall, and show her what a man could do to a woman if he had a mind to. He wanted to take her, use her, and discard her.

He sighed. Unfortunately Mrs Carlisle had appointed her as his Sister-in-Charge, and instead of

executing these pathetic fantasies on her improbably
unresisting form, he had to prepare himself to
encounter her daily in the operating theatre. 'Retrac-
tors, Sister, please.' 'Good morning, Sister. All
ready?' That was to be the intercourse between them.
He had to hold her at arm's length, survey her with a
cool eye. Daily. Or, to be precise, four days a week,
Monday to Thursday inclusive. From Friday to eight
a.m. on Monday, of course, she'd be at home at
Field End with that father of hers, that strange and
likeable man whose life was hanging in the balance.
Who was his friend and his patient. In other words,
he wouldn't even be free of the girl at weekends.
He'd be struggling, with her as his inevitable partner
again, to bring her father to his senses, to make him
accept treatment before it was too late. Another
situation in which it would be unthinkable to use her
in the way his fantasies urged.

He shrugged broad shoulders impatiently. This was
a storm in a tea cup. No need to make heavy
weather. He'd seen Alix for the first time looking like
some yob's sex object. That, apparently, was how she
chose to look when she wasn't on duty. Well, it was
up to her. Nothing to do with him. Nothing whatever.
The fact that her appearance had misled him
hopelessly on that first occasion was no fault of his.
Quite the contrary. She had a sexy body, she'd
flaunted it at him, and he'd responded in a normal
way. An entirely normal way.

What he'd felt was a brief and passing physical
infatuation. Nothing more. Infatuation always passed,
leaving nothing whatsoever behind. That was how it
was going to be with Alix. That was how he was
going to see it would be. There was nothing he could
do to get out of having her around. He couldn't, for
instance, turn on his heel now, this minute, go back
and tell Mrs Carlisle that, sorry, he'd thought it over,

and he couldn't approve her candidate for the post. He didn't want Alix Rutherford as Sister-in-Charge. Mrs Carlisle must look for someone else.

He had to accept reality. Alix had been appointed. He was going to treat her with rigid professionalism. He was landed with her, but he could handle it. Scowling, he set his shoulders, turned away from the window and walked through to Intensive Care. He did a round of the new admissions, including Kevin Neal, still in a precarious condition, spoke gently and as hopefully as he dared to Mrs Neal, nearly as white-faced as her husband, and then went along to the thoracic ward for his round there. They found him exceptionally impatient and fault-finding. They signalled protests to one another across the beds, elevating pained eyebrows, casting eyes upwards towards the ceiling in martyrdom, darting knowing glances. At last, after his broad back had stalked stiffly away through the double doors, they were able to discuss him openly.

What could have got into him?

He'd been called to the accident unit, of course, in the middle of outpatients. A stove-in chest and a ruptured spleen. But the patient hadn't died on the table. On the contrary, he was safely in Intensive Care.

Afterwards there'd been the appointment with Mrs Carlisle. That must be it. They'd had a bust-up about the day surgery centre. Eyes gleamed at the prospect of a hospital feud in the making.

Walking out to his Volvo, Jo himself was astonished to discover that his ideas about Alix's appointment seemed already to have changed. His anger had dissipated. He felt more like an excited boy planning to meet a new date. A blind date. That, he decided, unlocking the driver's door, described the situation rather well. Because he hadn't the faintest notion what to expect of Alix.

Or himself, for that matter.

Would she bring her purple hair and her sexy walk to St Mark's? No, of course she wouldn't. The evening they had had dinner at Long Barn after the play, she'd been wearing a scarf to hide her hair. She'd said so. It had been Daniel who'd told her to remove it. In fact, now he came to think of it, at that moment he'd had a glimpse of a different girl. She'd been unsure of herself, uncertain, on edge. He remembered it clearly. Immediately afterwards, though, he remembered with even more clarity, going downstairs to the restaurant, she turned into a sex-pot again.

And this was his new Sister-in-Charge. How was he ever going to deal with her?

He was down to play chess with Daniel tomorrow. And he'd said he'd do the lung function tests. He couldn't get out of that. She'd assist him, they'd have to work together then. What's more, he'd have to admit he knew about her new job. He'd no option. He'd have to say something politely welcoming about it, pretend to be pleased. Daniel would expect it.

She brought nothing but problems, Alix Rutherford. A pity she wasn't safely back in the Central, out of the way, unable to disturb anyone.

When he arrived at Field End, she opened the door to him. He was carrying, she noticed at once, the equipment for the long function tests. So he'd remembered his promise. Marvellous of him. All she said, though, with the utmost formality—they might have been about to embark on one of the more starchy consultant rounds at the Central—was 'Good afternoon, Mr Standish. Do come in. My father's expecting you.'

'Thank you.' He was thrown. She didn't look in

the least like the image of her he'd been carrying so unwillingly around in his head. Her dark hair close to her small skull, wearing shabby jeans and a washed-out shirt, she was a wisp of a girl. 'Before I see your father, Miss Rutherford, I must just say how—' how what? Oh, come on, a minimum of courtesy, that's all. He could rise to a phrase or two of conventional politeness to a new member of staff, couldn't he? He'd done it often enough. Come on. '—how delighted I am to learn you'll be joining us as Sister-in-Charge next week.' He paused, duty done, and Alix opened her mouth to reply, but he went on. 'I think,' he added, and the words came grinding out as if he grudged every one of them, as of course he did, 'I think we all realise how fortunate we are to be able to appoint a Sister from the Central's theatres to our very new centre.'

Alix had never been slow, and she could hardly fail to understand that what he was signalling was the reverse of what he was saying. Obviously, for some weird reason—had he a girl-friend he'd wanted to have the post? That must be it—he resented her appointment. She gave him one of her rare pebble looks from stony grey eyes. 'I wouldn't have dreamt of taking it,' she said unforgivably, 'if it hadn't been for my father's health.'

'Then it's a case of no cloud without a silver lining, isn't it? For clearly we at St Mark's must regard your appointment in that light.' Smooth as silk, but Alix was well aware that he would prefer to have demolished her. Reduced her to pulp.

What failed to occur to her was the form this would have taken. She knew nothing of the barbarian trying to escape Jo's control. That he had any sort of urge to take her slight frame and grind it into the ground never occurred to her. She hadn't yet grasped that he even knew what she looked like. She was, she assumed, simply Daniel Rutherford's daughter, to whom he had to be routinely polite.

What did occur to her, and with a good deal of force, was that Mrs Carlisle would be shocked to hear her newly appointed Sister-in-Charge from the Central quarrelling childishly with her chief before she'd even taken up the post. This was the road to disaster. She had promised Mrs Carlisle to run the Day Surgery Centre, and this involved getting on with its staff. What she felt about this maddeningly fascinating man was neither here nor there. She certainly intended to keep it to herself. As far as he, and everyone else at St Mark's, was concerned, she was the capable, unruffled and good-humoured Sister-in-Charge. 'Of course,' she added, blandness personified, 'although I suppose it wouldn't actually have occurred to me to think of leaving the Central if it had not been for my father's health, you must understand I feel myself tremendously lucky to have this splendid opportunity to be in at the opening of your new unit. Sir.' That should do him.

It did. He didn't, of course, believe a word of it, but he recognised immediately the smooth teaching hospital recovery technique—and respected her for it. She'd demonstrated, as he might have guessed she would, that she had a proper sense of responsibility towards her new post. How she'd hated the phrases she'd forced herself to utter, though. Briefly, laughter lurked in his eyes, and his mouth quirked in a fashion entirely different from the sardonic twist he'd shown her a few seconds earlier. 'Thank you, Miss Rutherford.' He was as bland as she'd been herself. 'I'm sure we shall enjoy establishing it together.' He smiled affably, and led the way into the big living-room as if he were advancing into a ward full of patients.

Only one patient, of course. This damned girl's father. 'How are you, Daniel?'

'Fine, fine.' The patient was irritable, and lying like a trooper. He looked pale, tired and ill.

Now for it, Jo decided. He dumped the machine he'd been carrying on the floor by his chair, and addressed Daniel. 'Before our game, I thought it might be a good idea if I made some measurements of your breathing capacity. To know more about your lung function will be very useful to me in helping me to see the best way to get you in better shape than you are at the moment.'

The patient muttered ungratefully that he was perfectly all right. No need for all this fuss.

'You aren't all right.' Jo was short. 'You know it, I know it, and so does your daughter. You need investigating, I've told you so before, and this'll have to be done some time. Now or later. I can do it for you here, with this machine I've brought with me for the purpose, or you can have a hospital appointment and go to St Mark's one day soon. Up to you. Personally, I'd have it in the comfort of your own home, if I were you.'

Behaving almost exactly like his daughter a few minutes earlier, Daniel took hold of himself, and said with polite insincerity that it was very kind indeed of Jo to take so much trouble, and of course, as he'd been good enough to bring the necessary equipment, he would take advantage of his generous offer. 'What do you want me to do?'

'To breathe into this.' Jo put his machine up on the table where they usually played chess, opened the lid, unfolded the tube and fitted a new mouthpiece. 'I expect you know how to use one of these,' he said. 'You must have done it before.'

Daniel nodded. 'I have, yes. Not for some time, though. My bronchitis has been so much better for years now—I can't imagine why it should suddenly hit me like this.' He could guess why only too easily, and he was sure Jo could too, and no doubt Alix as well, with her training. Even so, he was not going to admit to either of them that he knew he was very likely not suffering from bronchitis at all, but from the effect of too much smoking, about which he'd been warned for so long.

Jo was setting up his equipment ready to record Daniel's breathing capacity, and spoke across it now to Alix. 'Miss Rutherford, I wonder if you'd be so good as to assist me?'

'Of course,' Alix said coolly, effectively disguising the way her heart had leapt with joy. 'What would you like me to do?'

'I was thinking it would be useful, after the first measurements have been made, to put in slow adrenaline while continuing the readings. That would enable us to check on how much of his present breathlessness is reversible. So would you give your father subcutaneous adrenaline for me? That would allow me to run a series of tracings.' He turned to the patient. 'The aim of all this, Daniel, is to find out, if we can, how much of your present breathlessness is due to spasm—which means it's reversible—and how much to permanent damage in your lungs. Once we know, we can plan treatment with far more confidence. And with your daughter here to assist me by giving you the adrenaline, we'll be able to measure the exact effect this has on your breathing. First of all, though, if you don't mind, I want to take your blood pressure.' He unrolled the sphygmomanometer cuff, took out his stethoscope. 'If you'd just roll up your shirt sleeve for me. Thank you.'

Alix had never seen Jo at work before, and she watched his face tauten into concentration as he listened through the stethoscope to the pulse in her father's arm, watching the dial. A wave of deep feeling surged through her, startling her by its intensity. She loved this man. She asked nothing more than to be able to devote her life to him for ever.

She must be right out of her mind.

'Thank you, that's quite satisfactory,' Jo said, though to Alix's disappointment he didn't choose to divulge what her father's blood pressure happened to be, merely unrolling the cuff from Daniel's arm, putting it away with the sphygmomanometer, and then asking her to prepare the site of the injection. When she'd done this, presumably to his satisfaction, he handed her the loaded syringe. 'All right?'

'Quite all right, thank you,' Alix responded with heavily overloaded dignity, though her heart seemed to be still singing its mad song. They were working together, she and Jo Standish, and life was brimming with promise. Ludicrously, she even began to believe that somehow, with Jo here, measuring her father's breathing capacity, Daniel's lungs would all at once prove to be healthy. She set her lips. Pull yourself together, Alix Rutherford. There are no miracles in this world, and nothing Jo Standish could do would alter the state of her father's lungs. Stop this crazy day-dream, watch the spirometer, and be ready to put in the adrenaline.

Jo turned to Daniel. 'Now I'm going to take the first readings,' he said. 'Then your daughter will inject the adrenaline. All right?'

'Quite all right. Ready when you are.' Daniel was terse.

'Here we go, then. Take a deep breath, hold it. And blow out. Thank you. Fine. And again.'

Alix watched the tracings pour out of the spirometer, until Jo turned towards her. 'I think now you could start putting in the slow adrenaline, Miss Rutherford.'

'I'm doing that—now.'

'Good. Thank you. This will have an effect on your breathing, Daniel, which I'll be able to measure, and we'll see it show up on the tracing, and this will tell us more about the condition of your lungs. It'll be most useful.'

They went through the same procedure again, until Jo called a halt. 'Thank you. I think we've got maximum improvement in the breathing, so stop putting the adrenaline in, will you, Miss Rutherford? That's the last time you'll need to blow into this gadget, you'll no doubt be relieved to hear, Daniel.' His eye traversed the tracings spilling out across the table. 'These aren't at all bad, these results. In fact at first glance I'd say they're rather hopeful.'

Daniel smiled palely. In some corner of his mind he'd half supposed that his own incompetent and feeble breathing into this apparatus of Jo's would finally demonstrate that his lungs were not only useless but failing fast. The apparatus would show he was on the point of death. Suddenly he felt a good deal better. It hadn't been so bad after all. He even began to experience a distinct sense of achievement. All he said, though, and that somewhat grumpily, was, 'Well, at least we've done it, if it has to be done. I suppose that's something. And Alix has made an appointment for me to have those additional X-rays at the hospital next week.'

'You have?' Jo looked at Alix, who nodded. 'Tuesday afternoon.'

'Excellent. I'm delighted to hear it. We do need, Daniel, to have a proper look at that spot. I want to know a good deal more about it, before we can decide on treatment.'

Daniel sighed, and rolled down his shirt sleeve. 'If you say so,' he agreed wearily. 'But that'll be it. After that I'm getting back to my book. No more interruptions until I've completed the first draft. I want to show it to my publisher. I'm not having any more investigations until after that. Alix is driving me to the hospital on Tuesday for these X-rays, and on Wednesday she's going up to London to clear out her flat, and while she's away I'm going to write non-stop, and then early the next week I've an appointment with my editor.' He frowned, and avoided Jo's eye.

This was not the moment to argue with him. Jo was certain of that. He'd try and see him at the hospital, he decided, when he had the tomograms, and pin him down to another appointment for a bronchoscopy. But for the moment he'd obviously had enough—in fact, it would probably do him more good than anything else to be able to get back to his book.

Alix had been watching them both. 'How about a cup of tea?' she suggested.

'What a splendid idea.' Jo was enthusiastic, every inch the hearty encouraging doctor.

'I must say, Alix, it's a great thought,' Daniel agreed.

'I'll make some.' She departed for the kitchen, while Jo began dismantling his equipment and stowing its bits and pieces away.

Daniel watched him. 'Jo, while Alix is out of the room,' he said suddenly, 'tell me, what are my real chances? This spot on my lung—do you think it's a growth? Is it going to be the end of me? That is what you think, isn't it?'

Jo took a deep and steadying breath. To lie or not to lie? To remove hope? 'I don't know,' he said slowly, feeling his way. 'It could be a growth, yes. In fact the chances are that it is, to be honest. But even that means that it may not be.'

'But you think it is?'

'I think it's, shall we say, more likely than not. But

we don't know. Not until we have a further look. It's not inevitable.'

'But if it is a growth, then it could spread?'

'If it is a growth, then the sooner we get it out, the less likely it is to spread. That's why I'd like you to cease these delaying tactics.' He smiled gently, patted Daniel's shoulder.

Daniel twitched angrily away from the would-be comfort. 'I've told you from the beginning that I'm not having this book interrupted. I'll have these X-rays on Tuesday, but that's it. After that I'm completing this first draft before I go near that damned hospital again.'

'All right. If that's how you want it. It's your chest, and your decision. As long as you know the score.'

'I do. You've made it plain enough.'

'You mustn't assume the worst is inevitable. There is, I'd say, a thirty per cent chance that what you have may not be a growth. So don't make up your mind you're doomed. You aren't. And in any case, even if it is a growth, you may still get away with it— I may be able to remove it, and it may never spread, or trouble you further. So try not to be despairing.'

Alix came in with the tea, and Daniel talked about his book until Jo put down his cup and saucer and rose to his feet. 'I think I'd better be off. You don't want a game of chess—you want your typewriter. I'll try and see you next Tuesday, when you come for the tomograms. If I haven't been called away for anything urgent, I'll meet you in the X-ray department.'

'That's awfully kind of you,' Alix said, following Jo towards the front door, while her father made wheezily off in the opposite direction, losing no time at all in retreating to his beloved workplace.

Jo sighed. 'I've lost this round,' he admitted. 'I couldn't push him any further, but I'm disappointed. I had been hoping to pin him down to a bronchoscopy at the end of next week. No joy, though. He was adamant he's going to finish this first draft, and see his publisher, before another hospital appointment. And I'm bound to say, the way he put it, I had to give in. He was talking about it while you were getting tea, and after what he said, I didn't feel I could push him any more today.'

'He's always been like this about his books.' Alix spoke with some exasperation. 'He says it's just this one that's so special, but it isn't, you know. Each book is special when he's writing it, and he won't ever allow anything to interfere, no matter how important it seems to everyone else. Can I ask you'— they were at the Volvo now, and she watched Jo stowing the Vitalograph away—'what did you think of his tracings?'

'Better than I'd expected, frankly. In fact, I genuinely do think the results are quite hopeful, as I told him, because the impairment to his breathing capacity does look as if it should be to a large extent reversible. I think he'd be fit for surgery.'

'You do? That's something.'

'I'd like to get him in better shape first, of course, but there's no point at present in urging him to rest, or do regular breathing exercises, or anything like that. He'd just tell me to get lost.' Jo smiled, a wry and endearing smile that Alix drank in hungrily, and settled himself into the car, adjusted his seat-belt. 'Thank you for your assistance,' he said formally, transformed instantly back into the busy consultant surgeon out on a domiciliary call, so that Alix's spirits, which had momentarily climbed wildly skywards, collapsed into the ground at her feet. 'Invaluable,' he added. 'I hope to see you at St Mark's on Tuesday, then.'

'It's very good of you to spend so much time and thought on Dad and his problem,' Alix said with all the cool politeness she was able to summon. 'I appreciate it, even if he doesn't.' She smiled, a heartrending smile, Jo found it, and he drove away down the lane thinking not about Daniel and his damaged lungs but about a slight, tired-looking girl in jeans who was going to be his Sister-in-Charge.

CHAPER SEVEN

St Mark's Hospital

On Tuesday afternoon Alix unearthed her father from his writing room, persuaded him, through muttered grumbles, downstairs and into the Porsche, and drove him to St Mark's.

He sat hunched in the passenger seat saying nothing, and she assumed at first that he was sulky and put out at being separated from his book, and was, as so often, doing his utmost to lose himself in his characters despite this tiresome interruption of a hospital appointment. It wasn't until they were going through the doors into Outpatients, and she indicated the turning leading to the X-ray department that she caught his fear.

Her father was afraid. She was twenty-four, a trained nurse. She was thoroughly used to anxious patients, accustomed to reassuring them. Yet it had never crossed her mind that her own father might be afraid. She had let him down. She could so easily have helped him during the drive to the hospital from Field End, but it simply hadn't occurred to her that he might be in any need of support.

She took his arm. 'Nothing to it, Dad, you'll see,' she assured him, in a warm and loving voice he'd never heard from her before. Arm in arm, they walked along the corridor, and then, unexpectedly, a door opened and through it came Jo Standish.

'Good God,' he said. 'Here you are. Bang on time.

95

I might have guessed it—I was just coming out to the car-park to meet you.' He led the way back along the corridor into the X-ray department, where he introduced Daniel to the radiographer, and then Alix, too. 'Sister Rutherford, who as you've probably heard will be working here from next Monday as my Sister-in-Charge. Are you staying, Sister, or do you want to be off?'

'I'd like to stay, if I may.'

'By all means. Glad to have you with us. Now, Daniel, if you'd like to strip to the waist, here, in this cubicle—all right?'

'All right, thanks.' Daniel was curt.

Alix took the opportunity of this brief disappearance behind the curtain to move away and hiss at Jo, jerking her head towards her father. 'He's petrified. It never occurred to me that he might be, but he is.' The great grey eyes, no longer stony, met his and begged him to do something. Anything.

'Stay with him, then, and help to position him.' Jo was matter of fact, and no one could have suspected what he was feeling.

'Can I? I would like to.'

'Rosemary will be quite happy about it, I'm sure.'

'Of course, Sister. Please do.'

'Perhaps you'd like to begin by collecting him, eh? He should be about ready now.'

In the cubicle, when she pulled the curtain back, Daniel looked nervy and unhappy, but his face lit up when he saw Alix. 'They're ready for you now, Dad.'

'I'm glad you're going to stay,' he told her, in an abrupt, bitten-off voice that succeeded in sounding a good deal more angry than pleased.

Alix helped him on to the couch, while the radiographer positioned the equipment over him, and made a trial traverse.

Jo joined them. 'What we're going to do,' he told

Daniel, 'is take pictures of your chest at different depths, so that we can get a better idea of exactly where this spot of yours is. Each time Rosemary takes a picture, she'll have a specific depth in focus, while the detail above and below will be blurred out. So the machine will keep on orbiting over you until we have the required number of pictures. All you have to do is lie there while Rosemary takes them. She'll ask you to take a deep breath, and hold it, and all you have to do is just that.'

'When the picture is actually being taken,' Rosemary added, 'you'll hear a whirring noise. Ready? Right. Here we go. Take a deep breath, hold it.' The machine whirred and orbited, there was a clunk as the first picture was taken. The process was repeated until she said, 'That's it. Last one. You can relax now. Are you going to wait for the films, Mr Standish?'

'I would like to have a quick glance, before we let the patient go, if you wouldn't mind, yes.'

'Right, I'll take them through, then.' She disappeared into the dark room.

'Just stay as you are, Daniel, would you, while the films are processed? I think we've got enough for what we want, but I'll just have a look at them to make sure, and then if we need to take another I shan't have to ask you to come in again for a separate appointment.'

Daniel, quite chirpy by now, grinned cheerfully. 'Anything that saves me giving up another afternoon is OK by me,' he said, and lay on the couch under the great machine looking, to Alix's astonishment, almost relaxed.

'How's the book going? Still hoping to finish it by the weekend?' Jo asked.

'I think so, yes—with any luck, and provided nothing goes wrong. Alix is going up to London tomorrow for a couple of nights, so while she's away I intend to work non-stop. I'm hoping to finish it by the end of the weekend—no chance of any chess, I'm afraid—and then next week I'll read it through and make any necessary corrections and alterations. If all goes well, it'll be ready to take up to my editor on Thursday—anyway, I've gone ahead and made an appointment to have lunch with her then. I'll stay at my club overnight, go to the London Library on Friday, and then back home.'

This entire programme was news to Alix, and she listened with interest.

Jo turned to her. 'You'll be back from London, I gather, in time to come to our final committee before the opening of the Centre?' He sounded both disbelieving and threatening, Alix thought, and she imagined what he was in fact saying was 'Don't go mad socialising in London and overlook the Friday committee.'

'I shall be there.' She was crisp. He seemed to suppose her to be some sort of feckless child, irresponsible and forgetful, she thought despairingly. Would he never get round to thinking of her as an adult—a capable adult, too, and good at her job. Well, she'd have to show him. She would have been staggered to learn that his enquiry had been prompted by a longing to check on when it would be that he'd see her again—Daniel having put paid to his earlier hope of meeting her at the weekend.

The radiographer came back with the newly-dried pictures.

'Ah, here we are,' Jo said. 'Thank you, Rosemary. Now let's have a look and see what we've got. Very nice. Good. Exactly what I wanted. It shows up very well. Care to have a look, Daniel?'

It was plain from Daniel's expression that there was nothing he desired less, but he stepped obediently

across the room and peered at the films displayed against the lighted screen.

'Just there,' Jo said, pointing with his pencil. 'You see that darker shadow, and close by that circular patch? That's it. That's what we have to get at. It would be about *here*.' Unexceptedly, he swivelled round and prodded his pencil into Daniel's chest.

His patient retreated hastily. 'I accept your word for it,' he said shortly. 'All right if I get dressed? No more pictures? Then I'll be off.' He backed towards the cubicle, where he could be observed—he didn't wait to pull the curtain across—dragging on his shirt and scowling.

'Thank you very much for all you've done,' Alix said. She knew how much Jo had put himself out—Daniel had had the red carpet treatment, though he seemed totally unaware of it.

He came out of the cubicle in a rush. 'Thank you for all your trouble. Most appreciative. And I look forward to another game of chess after I've got the book off, eh? Alix, we really must—we should be—time is getting on, and . . .' His voice floated back indistinctly as he puffed wheezily down the corridor towards home and the security of his writing room.

'Thank you again,' Alix said, and hared after him.

They went through the main outpatient hall, out to the Porsche, and drove home to Field End in silence, both of them thrown by the events of the past half-hour. Daniel, who had imagined himself to be fully aware of the implications of his illness, had discovered that he had not really, whatever he might have informed Jo, actually believed in the existence of this patch on his lung. Now he did. He hadn't actually been able to see any difference between one dark blob and another on the films Jo had demonstrated to him, but he did accept that these films were pictures of his own chest, taken as he lay there on the couch, and that the damage to his lungs was there, visible to Jo if not to himself.

One of those patches was very likely going to kill him in the near future, if he didn't allow them to do something about it. This was what Jo had said the other day. This was why Alix had suddenly thrown up that job she'd been so pleased about.

When Jo had jabbed him in the chest with his pencil and said 'It would be about here', Daniel at last had to accept that this growth was somewhere inside his own lungs, not just a technical patch on an X-ray. It might be spreading with every breath he took.

He was worried stiff. But he was confirmed, too, in his original decision. The book was what mattered. The book had to be finished, at all costs. If time pressed, then he must work harder, and faster. Because he was going to finish it before he died. It looked as if it was the best thing he'd done, and if it had to be his only memorial, at least it would be one he could be proud of. So he was damned if he was going to be admitted to St Mark's, for Jo to extract great chunks of his lung, and then droop about afterwards for months feeling half dead. That was no way to finish the book of his life

Alix felt nearly as bad. From the moment that Dr Lomax had first broken the news of Daniel's probable diagnosis to her, she'd harboured few doubts. But today, seeing the tomograms, seeing the little intrusive dark patch demonstrated, and her father standing there with his shirt off, she felt despairing.

As they drove back to Field End, she wondered what on earth she could say to him. He was upset. He sat next to her, frowning, silent, rigid with barely controlled anxiety.

Her instinct was to be comforting, to treat him like a beloved child more than a father. She wanted to hug him, tell he'd be all right, just leave it to Jo. She wanted to lead him to his chair by the fire, pour hot tea into him, make him dripping toast or hot buttery scones and cherish him lovingly.

That might be the wrong way to go about it, though. If she battened down her loving concern and instead went after him with all guns firing, bullied him into accepting the necessity for a bronchoscopy and even possibly immediate surgery, she might be doing him the best service she could. She might, just possibly, save his life.

She couldn't do it, though. She chickened out. He looked so weary and anxious that she simply gave him his tea by the fire, and allowed him his usual escape afterwards into the writing room. Today she couldn't grudge it to him. If he could succeed in forgetting the threat hanging over him by escaping into mediaeval espionage, she could only be thankful.

She despised herself bitterly, though, for what she thought of as her feebleness. She was allowing herself to evade the issue. Jo Standish would probably tell her she'd failed Daniel. This afternoon had been the psychological moment to work on him—and she dodged it. She might assure herself she couldn't bear to hurt her father when he was down, but in reality it was herself she couldn't bear to hurt. To have braced herself, waded straight in and told Daniel exactly what he was up against, no matter how much she hated doing it—that was what she should have done.

The next morning she had to leave for London to clear out her flat. By failing Daniel this afternoon, she had ensured that matters would drift on for another week.

She could go across now to his writing room, interrupt him and read the riot act.

She shook her head. No good. She wasn't made like that.

It would have to wait until she returned from London. At least then she'd be established down here, with as much time as she needed ahead of her to see to her father's problems. In fact, she reminded herself, it just might be a better policy. To go for him now, and then clear off to London for several days, leaving him alone and disturbed, wouldn't be exactly caring or supportive.

She couldn't cancel the London trip—there was a tenant waiting to take over her flat as soon as she emptied it of her belongings and handed over the keys.

She drove to London in the Porsche. Her father had pressed the car on her, pointing out that if she was going to clear out her possessions she'd need transport to bring them home, and she'd accepted gratefully.

Once she reached the flat a new attack of gloom hit her. This was her own place, and when she'd left here for her holiday her life had stretched invitingly ahead, her career planned, her days committed to the Central. When she'd left here she'd known nothing about her father's life-threatening condition.

She paid a duty call on Miss Frobisher to apologise at having let her down. 'It was very good of you not to ask me to work out my notice.'

'My dear, in the circumstances I wouldn't dream of it. Your place is down at Halchester with your father, as long as he needs you.'

Alix sighed. 'That's what I decided. But I hate leaving here.'

'I hate losing you. St Mark's are lucky to get you, and I told them so. But you're doing the right thing. I'm sure. And after all, you've found an interesting job. It will be good experience for you, to be in at the birth of a new unit.'

Alix thanked Miss Frobisher, and made her way

back along the corridors towards the front entrance. It seemed odd to have to accept that she was no longer part of this great hospital where she'd trained, where she knew, it sometimes seemed, almost everyone.

And here was one very familiar figure. Leo Rosenstein, of general surgery, who was to have been her chief if she'd been able to take up her post.

'Look 'oo's 'ere!' he bellowed—Leo was always the opposite of quiet and restrained. He took her by the shoulders and hugged her warmly. 'Nice t'see you, ducks. Sorry y'not goin' to be with us as we'd planned, though I dare say y'substitute won't be a total failure. In the circs, it's clear that where you're needed at present is at 'ome.'

Even if what he actually said was something they already know perfectly well, people were nearly always reassured by Leo's approval, and Alix was no exception. To hear her decision approved by him made her immediately feel confident of its inevitability, in a way she hadn't been until now.

'Y'look tired to death,' he went on, scrutinising her with those eyes of his that missed nothing. 'Suppose that's unavoidable, though. Take care of y'self as well as of y'dad, won't you? Remember, one of y'first duties is to keep y'self in good nick, eh?'

She nodded. He was right.

'Oo's lookin' after y'dad?'

'The—the thoracic surgeon at St Mark's,' she said. How would he take this? Would he turn down Jo Standish out of hand, say she must get her father straight up to the Central and one of their own pundits? If so, she'd be in deep trouble. 'Mr Standish,' she added, almost apologetically.

His reaction startled her. 'Jo?' he boomed, his voice thundering down the corridor. 'Y've got my lad, Jo, 'ave you? Good. You'll be all right with 'im. Couldn't do no better.'

'Yes, that's what I thought.' Alix was weak with relief. 'He—he seems—um—very good indeed.' The understatement of her life.

'Trained 'im m'self.' Leo chuckled, and patted her cheerfully on her narrow shoulder. 'Can't say more than that, can I? Eh?' And then, unexpectedly, the cheerfulness left him abruptly, and his face grew shadowed. 'He 'ad a hard time gettin' that post, overdue for it, and then some, but his career got blasted by that tragic marriage.'

For no reason she could understand. Alix went cold, and her eyes met Leo's with anguish.

Leo, never slow, saw a great deal more at that moment than Alix was ever to guess. 'Didn't you know about 'is marriage?' he enquired, and, turning, paced along the corridor with her towards the main entrance hall.

'No. I don't really know anything about him except that he's marvellous with Dad—and that he's fairly new at St Mark's, Dr Lomax said.' And that I have a good deal more than total confidence in him, that I'm probably, almost certainly, hopelessly in love with him, tragic marriage or no tragic marriage. Hopelessly. For ever. To the end of my days.

She must be right out of her mind.

'He married a patient with leukaemia,' Leo told her.

Alix's heart contracted, and for the first time since meeting Jo, she experienced a pang of poignant tenderness for him. She longed, too, to be able to do something, anything, to relieve the pain he must have endured. Until now, she'd been conscious only of her own emotions, her own need of him. Now she felt a surge of protective love, a desire to hold him in her own arms and somehow make it all up to him. All the pain. All the agony. Her comment to Leo, though, was flat. 'Of course, she must have died. How dreadfully sad.'

Leo was not taken in. He received her remark as what it actually was, a question. 'Yes, she died. It was inevitable, and 'e knew that before 'e married 'er, natch. We all knew it, and we were all against 'im marrying 'er. But 'e went ahead, and then 'e paid the price. And of course the price turned out to be higher than 'e'd bargained for. That's 'ow these things usually turn out, and they did for 'im, poor devil. It all went deeper than 'e'd known anything could go, if you ask me, and 'e suffered accordin'. Still does, in my opinion, for what it's worth.'

'I'm sure,' Alix agreed blankly. She saw herself now as useless. Inadequate. Inexperienced. Immature. Madder, in fact, than she'd already suspected, and certainly no fit partner for Jo Standish with his tragic history. He knew what real suffering meant. And real love, too. Her own love affairs dwindled by comparison into triviality. Herself and David Hurst, for instance—what a load of nothing that had been.

'I argued as strongly against 'is course of action as anyone,' Leo told her. 'He was my houseman at the time, and I said 'e needed 'is 'ead examining if 'e went ahead with 'is daft project.' He laughed shortly. 'But 'e paid not the slightest attention. Bound to admit, the experience, 'ard as it was, was good for 'im in the long term. Matured 'im. I 'ad to stand by and watch Jo turn from a boy into a man, before me eyes. It made 'im a better clinician, of course. And left 'im with a capacity for caring for patients as people, instead of as passing cases for surgery. And then 'e 'appens to be an extremely able surgeon.'

From Leo, this was high praise.

'Y'r father's in the best 'ands. Rely on it. Well,

mustn't keep you. All the best, ducks—and to y'dad,
of course. Keep in touch.'

'Oh, I will. And thank you.'

Alix walked out of the main entrance to the
hospital and across to her flat in a daze of jumbled
emotions.

On one point, though, she had no doubts. The
Central was behind her. Ahead lay St Mark's, and
Jo.

On this heady confidence, she picked up the
telephone and rang round her friends, inviting them
to a farewell party. She rushed round to the baker,
the delicatessen and the off-licence, laying in a huge
stock of rolls, pâté and cheeses, with a few bottles of
wine to start everyone off.

Her friends poured in throughout the evening, as
they came off duty, with bottles under their arms and
enough pot plants to stock a nursery.

What was she up to? What was all this about her
father? And why had she turned down her new post?

She explained about her father and St Mark's,
though not about Jo Standish. 'There are a few
advantages in the actual job, too,' she added. 'A
straight four days on, three days off, for instance.
And day duty only. It's on the coast, so I'll be able to
get in loads of swimming and sunning myself—I'll get
so tanned you won't believe it.'

'You're not tanned now,' a solicitous girl-friend
pointed out. 'You're pale, and you look more tired
than ever.'

Another ring at the door bell saved her from
replying.

It was David Hurst, the obligatory bottle under his
arm, a bemused expression on his face. 'I say, whose
is that super Porsche outside? Anyone here?'

'My father's, as a matter of fact,' Alix told him.

'*Your father's*?' He looked shattered. 'But it's the

ultimate machine—you never told me your father was *rich*.'

'He isn't. Just fairly comfortably off. And he likes cars.'

'Comforably off? With *that* in the garage?'

Alix began to wonder if their affair might have followed an entirely different course if David had known about the Porsche, and perhaps the exact state of Daniel's bank balance, from day one.

'Come in and have a drink,' she urged, feeling— ridiculously—a little guilty, because David already belonged to the past, and nothing he said really mattered at all.

Since he himself remained happily unaware of this, he spent what was left of the evening chatting her up, trying to grab a ride in the Porsche, and doing his best to fix a date when they could meet in Halchester on his next free weekend. He stayed until last, helped her to clear the room and wash up, and finally, after an abortive attempt to stay until morning, bade her a tender loving farewell, telling her he didn't know how he was going to exist without her.

'I dare say you'll manage to get along,' Alix said, and closed the door.

CHAPTER EIGHT

The Day Surgery Centre

PROMPTLY at eight o'clock on Monday morning the day surgery centre opened its doors to patients, and Alix took charge of her new department.

To her surprise her attitude seemed to be entirely different from her feelings when she'd been at the Central. There she'd always felt she was on trial. Here at St Mark's, she was brimming with confidence. She recognised the undoubted fact that they thought they were lucky to have her, and her morale was high from the first day.

Adding to its height, of course, was Jo's proximity. Working alongside him was exciting. To know he was around the hospital and might walk in to the little day centre operating theatre or to her own office added a zest to her routine that startled her by its intensity.

Unfortunately, however, Jo himself appeared to be the sole individual at St Mark's totally unaware of their enormous luck in having landed splendid Sister Rutherford from the Central. He took nothing for granted. Instead, he apparently expected her to prove her competence to him.

Who did he think he was?

True, she herself did happen to harbour a number of incredibly silly delusions about him, but these would wear off as soon as she grew used to him. She knew they would. They'd better. In the meantime she

108

was not going to allow St Mark's to watch a Sister from the Central turning herself into a doormat for any surgeon. Naturally she would be courteous and polite—hardly straying so much as a centimetre from the path of rigid formality demanded of senior sisters at the Central somewhere around 1880—but she'd show Mr Jo Standish what was what and who was who.

That the distant grandeur of her greeting each morning unnerved him to the point of incoherence she never guessed. He appeared to her merely correct and withdrawn. During the day, though, she'd often notice him snatching quick undercover glances at her—presumably, she decided, disliking what he saw and resenting her presence in charge of his centre. He often snapped, too. He was curt. Abrasive. Demanding.

But then all surgeons were like that on occasion, she reminded herself. And he was teaching as well as operating, for the centre was to be a training ground for junior staff in the workaday techniques that formed its staple activity. Teaching juniors always made surgeons acerbic, and they were forever asking loaded questions to trap the unwary. It was all in the day's work. She'd enjoyed it at the Central, so why not enjoy it now?

The answer, to her fury, came back loud and clear. Because this was Jo Standish cutting her down to size.

When she left Field End each morning in the Porsche—which her father had lent her while he was busy with his book—she never knew who she was going to find at St Mark's. An abrasive, fault-finding chauvinist, or a gentle soul emanating nothing but tender loving care to all around him.

Either way, of course, she loved him. But this awkward—and, she told herself firmly, merely temporary—fact she kept to herself. From her cool smile and detached attitude, anyone might have supposed her to be almost on the verge of boredom with the new job.

Boredom? She was exhilarated! From the second she arrived until the moment she left, she was on cloud nine and zooming.

Today, she completed her first week. It was over. The first week of working with Jo at St Mark's.

She unlocked the Porsche, only to realise that Jo himself was approaching across the car-park and making for her. What on earth could he want? Had she left something undone?

'I want to talk to you,' he began as he approached— an opening with which she had become familiar during the past four days. His next phrase, though, was entirely new. 'How about a drink? Got time for one before you go home?'

Had she time? For ever. As much as he wanted, any day, any hour. 'I think so,' she said crisply, consulting her watch as if she was having a problem fitting in the break with routine. 'I don't see why not.' Hardly an ecstatic response.

Jo was dashed. 'We can walk across to the Lamb,' he suggested tentatively. 'Unless you'd care to go further afield?' A moment ago he'd had hopes of taking her down to the harbour, to the Dolphin on the quayside, but already he'd lost confidence in that plan. She was behaving exactly as she'd done each day in her office, with never more than a quick minute to spare for him.

'The Lamb would be fine,' Alix said hastily. He sounded curt and impatient—clearly they'd better go to the nearest pub as fast as possible. And the Lamb was already familiar—each day as she drove in and out she passed it, an old coaching inn, long and low, with casement windows and a sagging roof of lichened tiles.

Inside there proved to be exposed beams, low ceilings, and half the staff of St Mark's recuperating from the rigours of the working day. Jo established Alix at a small table and disappeared into the throng for their drinks, saying briefly, 'Guard the table. Repel boarders.'

He was back amazingly quickly, shouldering through the melée with her white wine and a pint of some dark brew for himself. Sitting down opposite her, he plunged at once into the reason for their meeting. 'What I wanted to discuss was, how about getting your father along for his bronchoscopy next week? Do you think he'd wear the idea?'

So that was what it was. She'd been expecting him to launch a complaint about the way she was running the centre, while all the time he'd been thinking about her father. In the midst of his preoccupations with the opening of the centre, on top of all his other work, he hadn't forgotten Daniel. She felt weak with love and something appallingly close to adoration, but she pushed her own reactions hastily away. 'Tuesday,' she said precisely, 'is for chest cases, we decided.'

'Do you think he'd come?'

'I don't know.' The guilt she'd experienced earlier returned, redoubled, unbearable. 'I did plan to sound him out, and then I was going to ask you if you could fit him in, but I'm afraid I didn't get around to mentioning it. He was so wrapped up in finishing his book that I didn't like to bring it up.'

'Has he finished it yet?'

'Oh yes. Bang on time—though he's been up most of the night, I think. But he's taken it up today to his editor. He's spending the night at his club, going to the London Library tomorrow morning, and coming back tomorrow afternoon.'

'So he'll be at home over the weekend, and no book around?'

'That's right. He won't know what to do with himself without it, I don't suppose. He'll be like a cat on hot bricks, waiting to hear what his editor thinks of it. He's always jumpy at this stage, and this year it'll be worse. He's worried about this book, and not at all sure his publishers are going to approve of the new line.'

'Well, if you think it'll help I'll come over on Saturday and play chess with him. That should divert his thoughts. And we might fix the bronchoscopy at the same time—both of us work on him, eh?'

'If you could spare the time, that would be perfect.'

'Of course I can spare the time.'

Now Jo sounded every inch the senior surgeon again, after having been so nice. Somehow she must have offended him.

'Tell you what,' he added. 'How about the two of you coming out to Long Barn and having dinner with me, after the chess? Then we could finalise our arrangements over a meal.'

He couldn't have been offended after all. She must have been mistaken. What on earth was she going to do if her father wouldn't co-operate? 'That would be marvellous. I just hope Dad proves amenable, that's all.'

'I've handled more difficult cases than your father.' Jo was dry.

'Of course you must have done, many times, 'Alix agreed hastily. She'd boobed again. Why couldn't she handle this incredible man the way she would have handled any of them at the Central? She'd had few problems then. But she knew the answer only too surely. Because she cared too much. Jo was different from any other man she'd ever known, and meant more to her.

What an idiot she was being. For him she hardly existed, other than as his new and still suspect Sister-in-Charge, and the daughter of a patient.

He was involved in her father's management, though, so she could at least go ahead and consult him over a point that had been worrying her. 'There is something I'd be grateful to have your advice on,' she said.

'Go ahead.'

'I was wondering whether to ring Dad's editor, while he's safely out of the way in the London Library, and ask her not to be too quick about returning his draft. That would give us a better chance of doing the bronchoscopy—we shan't have a hope if she wants to see him early in the week.'

'That's true,' Jo agreed.

'On the other hand, it seems a bit treacherous to blow the gaff about his illness. I don't think he'd like his publishers to guess there's any sort of query about his fitness. However, he's very fond of Celia—his editor—and I don't think he'd necessarily mind her knowing—except that she might pass it on, mightn't she?'

'Very likely, I'd say. But I see no particular problem there. Why not simply say he's exhausted? After all, this editor must surely have seen that for herself—you hardly need to be qualified in medicine to spot the obvious fact that Daniel's worn out, and I see no reason why she should imagine anything more serious behind it.'

'You're right. That's it. I'll ring her and say he's been up half the night for weeks, finishing the book, and as soon as he gets it back he'll be the same again, so could she hang on to it for long enough for him to catch up on his sleep and get some fresh air

and exercise. That should do it. Thank you so much,
that solves it—I've been worrying a bit about whether
to spill the beans or not, but you're quite right, I
don't have to.'

Once he'd written this girl off as uncaring. 'Think
nothing of it,' he said easily. 'Another drink?' Another
drink, my beloved? Anything I can get for you,
anything I can do for you, only let me know. I'm
yours to serve for ever.

Hastily Alix drained her glass. He meant they'd
settled their business, and she should be off. He was
a busy surgeon, with not only the new centre to look
after, as she had herself, but the accident unit too,
and numerous private patients like her father scattered
round the countryside. 'No, thank you. That was
lovely. I must be off now, though. Thanks terribly for
all the advice. And I look forward to seeing you on
Saturday afternoon when you play chess with Dad.'
Still babbling incoherent thanks, she rose to her feet
and fled from the Lamb, along the lane, into the car-
park at St Mark's, and across to the Porsche.

Jo didn't follow her. She had walked away from
him, head high, without a backward glance, and he
had picked up unmistakable echoes of 'the purpose of
our meeting is accomplished. That's it. Thank you
and goodbye.' He was a useful colleague, able to
help her with that father about whom she worried so
much, but that was the end of it. Apart from Daniel,
and her job at St Mark's, he might as well not exist.
Someone back at the Central held her heart and all
her thoughts, that was what it must be. Only to be
expected, after all. A girl like that. Obviously there
wouldn't be an empty space in her life, waiting for
him to appear and claim it. Ridiculous.

Both of them spent a lonely evening. Alix alternated
yearning hopelessly for Jo with worrying about Daniel.
What was she going to feel after the bronchoscopy,

when they knew the worst? Madness to expect Jo somehow to find a way to save Daniel, so that he could write happily away for another twenty years.

Secretly, in her depths, she did cherish exactly this lunatic hope. It had been buoying her up ever since she'd known the probable diagnosis. Jo would see her father all right. But Jo was a busy surgeon, not a miracle worker. Her faith in him was misplaced. He could remove the diseased portion of Daniel's lung, but there was no chance whatever that he could, by the mere force of his personality, transform that dark patch she'd seen for herself on the tomogram into a nothing. She must face up to facts. Her father was very likely dying, and nothing she or Jo could do would prevent the inexorable advance of his disease.

In the morning she rang Daniel's publishers. Celia had been his editor for four or five years now, and seemed to know exactly how to handle him—since she'd taken over, there'd been none of the previous upsets and confrontations over his drafts. He and Celia worked on them together; Celia managed to insert suggestions and opinions without enraging him—rather the opposite, in fact, as he came away from a session with her tired but invigorated, eager to press ahead with new ideas and alterations. Celia understood his writing and what he was aiming at, he told Alix. She had a positive and creative attitude, and her confidence boosted his own.

Celia was the sort of person who did inspire confidence, of course. She looked as capable as she undoubtedly was. Small and sturdy, with crisp greying curls cut close to her head and a wide encouraging smile above a square determined chin, she wore no-nonsense tweeds, cashmere and pearls, and well-polished brogues on her small and firmly planted feet. Daniel insisted here was a great deal of sensitivity and warmth hidden away behind her outer brusque competence.

When Alix rang she was put straight through, and Celia's cheerful tones came briskly down the line. 'Hullo, Alix, how are you? We don't seem to have met for ages—but I'll be down to see Daniel next week as I expect you know. Shall I see you then?'

'Actually, Celia, that's what I'm ringing about. Dad is a bit exhausted, you know, and—'

'He always does look absolutely whacked when he's just completed a first draft, of course, but I was a bit worried yesterday when we had lunch. He looked so totally drained and worn out—you're worried too, are you?' Her voice sharpened.

Alix backtracked fast. Daniel would be furious with her if she implied to his publishers that he was on the verge of a breakdown, especially when he was anxious for them to launch his new image. 'No, no Celia, don't get me wrong. I'm not *worried*, nothing like that.' So what was she supposed to be ringing up for? 'It's just exactly as you say, this book is extra important to him, he's been working flat out on it, often right through the night, and now he's absolutely flaked. What I was wondering was, do you think you could possibly be a bit slow about coming down here to discuss it with him? Because once he's got the draft back from you and heard what you think, he'll begin work again—no stopping him. So I thought if you and I could sort of hatch a plot to give him a break in spite of himself it might be a good idea.'

'Of course. Anything I can do I'll be glad to. Count on me. Daniel is very important to me, as a person as well as a writer, and if ever I saw a man who looked as if he could do with a couple of weeks in bed, it was Daniel yesterday. He looked *ill*.' Celia's voice rose, and for the first time ever Alix thought she sounded unsure of herself.

Hastily she stepped in with false reassurance. 'I think it's just that he's worn out and short of sleep,' she lied. 'What I was wondering was, could you tell him the draft's great, but you won't be able to come down to talk about it before the end of the week? Do you think you could do something like that?'

'Of course. No problem. I can easily postpone coming down until, say, Friday. How's that?'

'Marvellous. Thanks so much. You won't let on, will you? Dad would be furious if he knew I'd been on to you.'

'Not a word. Anyway, I'll be relieved myself to think he's having a bit of a break, because he really did look rather frail yesterday.' The anxiety was back in Celia's voice, though she went on without a pause. 'Say I come down on Thursday night to work on it on Friday, how would that be? That would give him nearly a week free.'

'Great.' They could do the bronchoscopy on Tuesday, and then they'd know the worst—but she'd face that when she had to. And at least Daniel wouldn't be able to advance Celia's arrival as a reason for not having the bronchoscopy. One step at a time. 'Thank you so much, Celia—I hope I haven't mucked up your week for you?'

'Not a bit.' Celia reverted to her usual cheerfulness. 'And you can tell Daniel I'm really thrilled with the first draft, and making plans hard.'

'Super. I'll see you on Thursday evening, then.'

The next afternoon Alix met her father at the station and drove him back to Field End to one of Woody's bumper meals of jugged hare with redcurrant jelly, gamey and pungent, followed by apple pie and a choice of Stilton, Camembert or Emmental, his favourite cheeses. But he ate very little, merely pushing his food around his plate in the manner she'd grown accustomed to.

Over coffee she tackled him about the bronchoscopy. 'Jo's coming to play chess tomorrow, and he'll discuss it with you himself. But it's just possible he could fit you in on Tuesday.'

Her father jumped, and frowned. Plainly he didn't like the plan. Alix could guess how he felt. One side of him wanted never to have a bronchoscopy at all, ever, while at the same time he knew that as the ordeal was inevitably approaching, it might be easiest to jump in fast and get it over.

'Of course,' she remarked, at the crucial moment— at last she was beginning to understand her father—'I can't promise anything for certain. Jo might not be able to fit you in at such short notice. Occasionally he can be a bit of a stickler.' And that was the truth. You are a bit of a stickler, my darling Jo.

Her ploy worked. Suddenly Daniel wanted to have the bronchoscopy. 'To have it while I have these few days free would be most useful—don't you think he'd take that into account, Alix? After all, I've talked to him about the book. He does already know about it.'

'That's right. He does. And it might make all the difference. Well, we can sound him out when he comes for chess, see how he reacts. By the way, we're both invited to dinner with him tomorrow night at Long Barn.'

'Really? That'll be pleasant.'

Alix didn't push her luck. She changed the subject, began asking her father how he'd got on in London, and he told her about the books he'd brought back from the London Library.

The next afternoon, when Jo was due, she cleared off for a walk along the cliffs, leaving the two of them alone together.

She returned, windblown and tousled, hungry and thirsty, to find her father had defeated Jo, but only after, he explained, a hard-fought game, and that he had already broached the possibility of a bronchoscopy while the draft of his book was still with Celia in London.

'A thoroughly sensible plan.' Jo backed him enthusiastically. 'Can't imagine why it never occurred to me before. The obvious thing to do. I thought Tuesday morning. How does that strike you, Sister?'

'Tuesday is for chest cases, we decided.'

'Quite so.' His eye met hers with never a glint. 'So how's that, Daniel? Tuesday morning? Before lunch?'

'Thank you, I'd be most grateful if you'd fit me in then.' Daniel seemed to mean it, too, Alix thought, as she poured tea. How understanding Jo could be with patients.

After tea, Daniel and Jo returned to the chess board to work out the finer points of a game written up in the *Times* from the recent national championships, while Alix went up to her room to change out of her track suit and into something more suitable for dinner at Long Barn. During her walk she'd devoted a good deal of thought to what to wear that evening, but she was no nearer a decision. Something sexy, to show Jo she was more than the competent Sister-in-Charge at the centre. On the other hand, during her working hours she wanted nothing so much as to have him grasp that this was exactly what she was, competent and capable, totally reliable too, not some irresponsible child promoted from the wards before she was ready. Her father, too, would have a fit if she turned up looking too sexy. Or would he? Would either of them even notice?

She sighed, and settled for safety first, climbing reluctantly into her useful little black dress with only the merest hint of cleavage. A go-anywhere dress. Now she looked like the great writer's correct daughter, a mere appendage, unobtrusive, dutiful.

She put out her tongue at the nonentity in the mirror, and brushed her dark hair wildly about all over her head, so that it stuck out like a cockatoo in a fit. Why shouldn't she ginger up her boring appearance with a provocative hair style again? She brushed her hair into spikes, upstanding and outrageous. That would make them both sit up!

The last time she'd gone to Long Barn sprang vividly into her mind. She'd had purple hair, and for an hour or two it had changed her personality. For years she'd been satisfied to be a serious-minded student nurse, then staff nurse and finally Sister at her teaching hospital. Then, for one brief evening, she'd found another self. A sexy, confident girl with new dreams and strange ambitions.

Well, why not? She'd done the career bit, now came the moment to attempt to discover the stranger within, who'd been struggling to get out—since when? When had this new, uncomfortable personality first made herself known?

Since she'd first met Jo. That was when it had all begun to happen.

Nonsense. Nothing more than an odd coincidence.

Who was Jo Standish, anyway? He happened to be the Surgeon-in-Charge of the day centre. All right. But she was the Sister-in-Charge, wasn't she? With her own distinct responsibilities, her own sphere of work. She was Jo's partner, not his submissive handmaiden.

At this point in her thoughts she discovered to her extreme irritation that there was not only one unpredictable personality inside her struggling for a new life, but two. As well as this new, emerging, confident character there was another girl who disagreed with all that, whose dreams were entirely different. A girl who wanted nothing more than to be a devoted and submissive handmaiden to Jo Standish for as long as he'd have her. For ever, if possible.

She had to snap out of this. How feeble could you get?

Compulsively, she began to brush her hair with ferocity, and all at once it settled rather fetchingly into a sideways drooping cockatoo.

She stared at herself. This was it. This was a break with her usual style, and much more dramatic, but suggesting poise rather than aggression, and somehow belonging to her and the little black dress. Not strident, no one could have called it that. Perhaps coolly fashionable.

So there she was. That would have to do. She fastened her father's twenty-first birthday present of a pendant diamond on a thin gold chain round her throat, reached for the beaded and embroidered evening coat Zoe had just insisted on passing on to her, and swept out of her room, along the balcony and down the open staircase. The confident stranger, unpredictable as ever, surfaced again, and though she didn't know it, she came down with a walk that startled Jo out of his wits. A slight, tired girl in a track suit, the hardworking Sister-in-Charge he'd just been telling himself he was growing used to, had gone upstairs a quarter of an hour earlier. Now, in her place, down strolled this riveting sex-pot in a slinky black dress with a glimpse of magnetising cleavage under some sort of heavily embroidered evening coat that shouted not only fashion but money as loudly as her walk yelled 'Want me? You may not get me.'

Bemused, he walked behind her into the restaurant at Long Barn. It was full of people from St Mark's, who greeted him. Some of them recognised Alix too. All of them began speculating instantly as to what part she played in Jo's life. Was there something on the go there? Eyes scrutinised them both in depth, traced the cleavage hungrily, and tongues wagged furiously as word went round that this was the new Sister-in-Charge of the day surgery centre, with her father—wasn't he a thriller writer, something like that?

Anyway, if Jo Standish was taking the father out as well as the daughter, no doubt of it, he must be serious about her.

CHAPTER NINE

Daniel at St Mark's

ON Monday evening Daniel was edgy, and ate even less than usual. He drank black coffee and smoked, and Alix hadn't the heart to stop him, though for weeks now she'd been telling herself that the instant his book was off his hands she'd tackle him about the absolute necessity of giving up his lethal little cigars. Not tonight, though. It wasn't the moment.

She wondered whether she should talk to him about the bronchoscopy. When they'd gone to St Mark's together for his tomograms, she'd wished she'd briefed him in advance. But a bronchoscopy was not as undemanding as a session in the X-ray department—would telling him about the procedure frighten him rather than reassure him?

She was undecided, and longed for Jo to be with them. He'd know how to handle her father.

Well, Jo wasn't here, and she was. So she'd better stop dithering and get on with it.

'Dad, is there anything you'd like me to tell you about tomorrow?'

He put his coffee cup down, eyed her oddly. 'Quite straightforward, isn't it? So you and Jo have been saying non-stop.'

Oh lord. She'd said the wrong thing. Now he was in one of his moods. She felt about ten years old, and nothing but a nuisance. Unexpectedly, though, within her someone else surfaced and took over.

Not a ten-year-old but a capable nursing sister of twenty-four. He was cross because he was frightened, and he didn't want to admit it.

'Of course,' she said. 'Absolutely straightforward. Jo's done hundreds of them. So, as a matter of fact, have I. Nothing to worry about at all. I just wondered if you might like a dummy run, so as to know what to expect.'

Daniel turned over the pages of the *Bookseller*, which he appeared to find engrossing, though Alix knew that in fact he'd finished reading it two days earlier. He shrugged nonchalantly, and remarked in a bored and offhand tone that he supposed there was no harm in being prepared, if she thought it useful.

'I'll be looking out for you when you arrive, and then we'll go along and join Jo.' On this comforting picture she had to pause for a moment. Join Jo, and all would be well. 'You'll already have taken that tablet Jo's left you when you get up—don't forget about not having any breakfast, will you? I've told Woody. When you get to the hospital Jo will very likely give you an injection, to relax you.' And are you going to need it, she thought ruefully. More than twelve hours to go still, and Daniel was jittery as hell.

'What exactly *is* this bronchoscope thing that goes down my windpipe?'

'It's a thin tube that functions like a telescope, for looking into your lungs. It's very flexible, and Jo will get a close-up of your air passages through it. Very likely he'll take a sample from your lung for the pathologist to examine in the laboratory, so that we know what that odd patch on the X-ray actually consists of, and can plan the best way of dealing with it.' Her thoughts raced ahead. Jo would do a biopsy, snip out a fraction of Daniel's lung tissue, the pathologist would look at it under the microscope, and tell them whether it was malignant or not. Or not? While there still remained a faint possibility that the patch would turn out to be benign, the chances were against it. The real question would be whether it was fast or slow growing, and whether it had already spread too far for them to be able to save him.

'It'll be cancer, won't it?'

'It's possible, Dad, yes. Equally, though, it might not be. It's important to find out as quickly as possible what it is, so that immediate treatment can give you a good chance of a complete recovery.'

'What sort of treatment?'

'That would depend on what Jo finds. Even if it was a growth—and we mustn't jump the gun, you know, it may not be—Jo might quite likely be able to remove it completely. And honestly, Dad, if you did need an operation, there couldn't be anyone better qualified to do it. Jo is unequalled. You're in absolutely the right hands.'

And that was nothing but the truth. Deluded she might be in loving Jo so much, but her assessment of his standing as a surgeon was correct. 'Anyway, it's still possible that you don't have a growth at all, simply a spot of infection or something like that.'

'You don't really believe that, do you? And neither does Jo.' Daniel's eyes, probing, were both challenging and fearful. He wasn't going to let her get away with a slick piece of spurious reassurance.

'We simply can't say, Dad. No one knows. That's why you're having the bronchoscopy.'

'H'mph.' He changed the subject abruptly. 'And how the hell does Jo get this blasted tube down into my lungs?'

'Through your nose, and then down your throat.'

This shook him. 'Through my *nose*? And then

down my *throat*?' He touched his nostrils, felt his neck. 'How can he possibly see down it, if it's small enough to go up my nose? And can he see round corners, or what?'

'It works, Dad, I assure you. It's a very thin tube with a wonderful optical system, costing thousands of pounds. Jo will anaesthetize your nostrils and the back of your throat, so you won't feel anything—though your throat may be a bit sore for a day or two afterwards. You'll need soup for supper, probably, and then yoghurt, or ice-cream, or one of Woody's fruit fools—anything of that sort.'

Daniel ignored this culinary diversion. 'A tube up my nose,' he repeated. 'And Jo looking through it into my lungs. The marvels of modern medicine, I imagine you call that, but I could do without anyone practising it on me, I must say. However, I suppose you both know what you're doing.'

'Of course we do, Dad. It's a routine investigation, and by this time tomorrow it'll be behind you.'

Daniel snorted. 'Thanks very much. What you actually mean is that by this time tomorrow some other horrible procedure, like an operation, will have taken its place. No need for all this pretence. I'm not a child. And let me tell you, Alix, I may have given in and agreed to have this blasted bronchoscopy, but I'm not having my book interrupted by any major surgery. If Jo decides the next step is an operation on my lungs, it'll have to wait.'

'We'll meet that problem if we have to,' Alix said. 'What's ahead of you now is simply a bronchoscopy. So how about an early night, take the tablet Jo's left for you, and I'll bring you some Horlicks in bed?'

A good deal to her surprise, Daniel agreed to this suggestion, and took himself off.

Alix made Horlicks and took it up to him. As she

climbed the stairs to the writing room, the strains of a Bach fugue floated down. Her heart sank. This was the tape he always played when he was in despair over a book.

Of course he was worried and depressed, she reminded herself sharply. For him to be anxious about what tomorrow would bring was normal. Realistic. To pretend to herself that anything she might do could remove all anxiety from her father's mind was futile. Daniel was in Jo's hands, tomorrow and afterwards, and clearly this fact brought him less reassurance than it did her.

Jo couldn't control what they were going to find, and that was what Daniel's future depended on. She must be out of her mind to be able to take comfort from the mere fact that it was Jo who would be responsible for the bronchoscopy.

Even so, whatever she might tell herself, to walk into the centre the next morning, and see his massive form standing foursquare in the entrance to her office only minutes after she'd reached it herself brought a wave of overwhelming relief. He remained throughout the morning session, too, teaching the pre-registration house surgeon from thoracic surgery to perform a deft bronchoscopy, while Alix instructed the student nurses.

'We'll just check, before we start, Nurses, the requirements for this procedure. First of all, a good light. Then a sterile towel, a sterile bowl half filled with sterile saline, sterile gauze squares, local anaesthetic jelly, biopsy forceps, sheathed brush biopsy apparatus, cleaning brush, glass slides and spray fixative, suction unit . . .' The list went on endlessly. She had laid out the trolley herself, she told them, but one of them would be expected to prepare it for the next patient.

All three of them looked slightly alarmed, though they chorused 'Yes, Sister,' dutifully in response.

The staff nurse brought in the first patient, and Jo and Don, the house surgeon, wearing sterile gowns and gloves, but not masks, converged on the couch. Jo explained to the patient what they were going to do, and then the bronchoscopy was under way. 'Breathe in through your nose, Mr Morris, while I use this little puffer.' He turned to the house surgeon. 'What do I have here, Don?'

'In the nebulizer, sir? Four per cent Lignocaine.'

'Correct. That's fine, Mr Morris. Now breathe through your mouth instead, while I direct this spray on to your throat. Excellent. Rest now. What next, Don?'

'We wait two minutes for it to act.'

'And then?'

'Then you do it again.'

'Right. Except that this time you can do it.'

'Thank you, sir.' Don repeated the spraying, and then Jo directed several more sprays of stronger Lignocaine to the patient's throat. 'Now I'm going to put this up your nose and repeat the procedure. Watch, Don. We spray as we withdraw the cannula, like this. Next the other nostril. All right, Mr Morris? What next, Don?'

'Wait two minutes.'

'Correct. And then we pass a single nasal cannula into the left nostril, for the oxygen. You fix that to Mr Morris's cheek, Don, will you, while I check the bronchoscope.'

Alix passed adhesive tape to Don, and informed Jo that she had inspected the bronchoscope and cleaned the lens.

'Good. Thank you. Now, Don, observe. I'm going to stand in front of Mr Morris, like this, and insert the bronchoscope into his right nostril, so. All right,

Mr Morris? Good.' Jo continued inserting the bronchoscope until he could begin to explore Mr Morris's bronchial tubes.

Alix tensed. On the X-rays, Mr Morris's shadow was very much like Daniel's. They were coming to the point where Jo would not only be able to see what the cause was in this patient's case, but where he'd very likely snip out a small piece of lung tissue and send it to the laboratory. Everything that was happening with Mr Morris was likely to be repeated when Daniel was the patient.

'Ah yes,' Jo said. 'Here we are. This is what we're looking for. Mmm. Yes, indeed. Come and have a look, Don.'

Don in his turn looked down the bronchoscope and made similar indeterminate noises. 'Mmmm. Yes, I see.'

'We'll do a biopsy now, Sister.' Jo's tone was brisk, and Alix failed to notice the warm sympathy in his dark eyes as he glanced briefly towards her—she was at that moment reaching for the biopsy accessories.

Jo took the first biopsy, but after this Don took two more. 'You need to apply exactly the right pressure to close the forceps, remember.'

Don lost his nerve, and snipped off too little.

'Never mind. We'll need another specimen anyway—we want at least three. Wash the forceps and start again. Press fractionally harder, but not hard enough to snap the forceps, and we'll have what we want. The correct pressure only comes with experience.'

Don tried again, and this time succeeded.

'Good. Now we've got what we need for the lab. I'm just going to have a final look round, Mr Morris, to make sure everything is as it should be, and then I'll remove the tube and you'll be through.

Afterwards you can have a rest here for a while—
Nurse will show you where—and then the ambulance
will take you home. Nothing to eat or drink,
though, before mid-afternoon, and particularly no
hot drinks until this evening. Until the local wears
off, you won't be able to judge hot or cold, and
you could scald your throat. When the laboratory
have had a look at these specimens we've taken, I'll
be able to go ahead and plan your treatment, and
I'll be in touch with you about the next step.'

The next step would be major chest surgery. Not
a doubt of that. He could see with the naked
eye that Mr Morris—another heavy smoker, like
Daniel—had an invasive type of growth. They'd
have to have him in, and remove at least a lobe of
his right lung. Now, though, wasn't the moment to
break the news to him. Mr Morris had been through
enough for one morning.

Don removed the bronchoscope, Mr Morris was
escorted to one of the cubicles to await the
ambulance, then Jo and Don repaired to Alix's office
for coffee, while Alix sterilized the bronchoscope and
the student nurses relaid the trolley.

One to go, and it would be Daniel's turn.

First, though, they had Mrs Prendergast, a
stout lady with wheezy, laboured breathing. The
bronchoscopy in her case was being done solely in
order to suck out her airways and help her to
breathe more easily. By comparison with Mr Morris'
prognosis, this was a nice cheerful result, and they
all felt a good deal happier when she departed than
they had done when Mr Morris had been taken to
his cubicle.

Now it was Daniel's turn.

In her Sister's blue, Alix walked through to
Reception, her head high, her white frilled cap
perched on top of her dark head, poised and

apparently brimming with confidence, every inch
the unflustered Sister-in-Charge. Inside she was
quaking. This was it.

She went to the big double doors, and saw Sam,
punctual as ever, drawing up in the Granada, Daniel
beside him.

As she went out to meet them, both their jaws
dropped. What on earth could be the matter with
them? They were expecting her, so what was so
astonishing about her appearance?

Sam came round the car to open the door for
Daniel, who had his eyes fixed on her, as if he'd
never seen her before. 'Here I am,' he said inanely.

'Absolutely on time. Splendid.' Alix heard her
own voice, over-hearty, too cheerful. Unconvincing.

'You don't half look smashing in that uniform,
Alix,' Sam told her, before returning to his own
side of the car. 'Real smart and efficient. Ever so
grown-up.'

At twenty-four that might surely be expected,
Alix thought, but evidently the idea was a shock to
her father and Sam, and presumably accounted for
the dropped jaws and glazed expressions.

'It's quite true.' Daniel put her thoughts into
words. 'You do look extraordinarily grown-up, my
dear. Only to be expected, I suppose—what it must
be, you know, is that, come to think of it, I've
never actually seen you in uniform. Most impressive.
I'm proud to be seen with you.' Now that the
moment of action was on him, he had himself well
in hand. He'd been jittery all morning, but here he
was, ready to face whatever fate threw at him. And
Alix was a bonus. He'd been glad to know that
she'd be with him, in any case, but he hadn't for a
second guessed that her uniform would change the
way he thought of her. She looked what she was,
part of this modern hospital, professional from the

top of her head to the soles of her highly polished shoes, and her presence was surprisingly confidence-building.

'In here,' she said, turning into a small room near the reception area.

And there was Jo, dressed up in a white gown, but not, thank God, one of those masks, coming to meet him.

'Here you are, Daniel. Come along in.'

Ridiculously, Alix's anxiety dissolved. Everything was going to be all right. Jo would see to it.

His personality dominated the small room and put a protective screen round both Alix and Daniel. Neither of them had any further worries. Alix didn't even stop to tell herself how silly she was being, that nothing had altered, that the worst could still happen, and within the next hour or two. She felt safe in Jo's enveloping care. What would come, would come, and when it did, Jo would be there beside her to see her all right.

She might secretly relax like this into his tender loving care, but as far as he and Don were concerned, she reminded herself firmly, she was Sister Rutherford, there to assist them impeccably, whether the patient happened to be her father or anyone else. Which was exactly what she was going to do. Unruffled, calm, she presided coolly over this third bronchoscopy of the morning.

Daniel was settled on the couch, his nose and throat were sprayed, Don put the oxygen tube up his left nostril, and finally Jo checked the bronchoscope, lubricated it, and inserted it into Daniel's nose.

This was it, Alix thought. Quite soon now they'd know the worst.

Whatever it might be, Jo would help her to handle it. And he would see her father through whatever surgery had to be undertaken. From Jo's bulky gowned form, so close to her, so close to Daniel, Alix drew confidence and support. This was not entirely her own fevered imagination, she knew. This was something Jo was genuinely able to do for patients and their relatives. Radiate reassurance and calm. Today she and Daniel happened to be on the receiving end, that was all. It meant nothing. It was just part of his job. And she was just a silly girl helplessly in love with her boss. The sooner she came to her senses, the better. But not now. She couldn't manage without him—and luckily she didn't have to, whatever the motives behind his support.

The bronchoscope had almost reached Daniel's vocal cords, and Jo put in more local anaesthetic, rotating the bronchoscope to attach the syringe. 'I'm just going to anaesthetize your vocal cords, Daniel, with this same local we used for your nose and throat. We'll wait a minute for it to act, while I have a look round, and watch your cords as you breathe in and out.' He looked down the bronchoscope. Alix held her own breath. 'Fine,' he said at last. 'Nothing amiss there. Everything moving as it should. I'll get Don here to have a look too, Daniel, if you don't mind.'

Don stared down the bronchoscope.

'You see the normal movement of the vocal cords? You need always to watch for inequalities of this movement, as it can be the first sign of recurrent nerve palsy. No sign of that here. Or anything else.'

Alix let her breath out. That was something. At least, as far as they had gone, everything was normal. No suspicious secondaries.

'Now I'm moving down into the larynx. I'm afraid this always takes a long time, Daniel, because we have to keep waiting for the local to work, so that I can move on. Here we go again, I'm looking at your trachea. Breathe in, out, yes, that's all very nice, everything working as it should.'

At last they reached the point where the anaesthetic went into the air tubes of the lungs themselves, and after the inevitable wait for it to take effect, Jo began examining the part of Daniel's lung that had looked ominous on the X-ray.

At any moment now, Jo might find the growth. He'd take a biopsy for the lab, and that would be it. They'd know the worst. Alix forced herself not to tense, somehow to remain calm. If she grew tense, Daniel would be sure to pick it up. She breathed slowly and regularly, willing herself into tranquillity.

'All right, Sister?'

The enquiry startled her. 'Quite all right, thank you, sir.' Her voice might be quelling, but her eyes were anguished.

There was nothing more Jo could say, but he sent all the love he felt across to her. Hold up, my darling. Keep going, my love. If I could only live through this agony for you, I would. If I could hold your hand and pour what strength I have for bearing disaster into you I would. But I have to concentrate on the bronchoscope and your father's lungs, and leave you to shoulder your own burdens. If only I could take them from you. All I want in life is to be able to love you and help you.

Could this be true?

Undoubtedly it was. Jo searched Daniel's bronchial tree and knew himself helplessly in love with Daniel's daughter.

Had that actually happened, Alix was asking herself? That look Jo gave her, when all at once his eyes had poured love into her, when it had seemed almost as if he had pressed his own body against hers, imbuing her with strength—had they been as close as that, for those few moments?

She knew they had. That look he had given her had been no accident, no trick of the imagination. He had meant it. He had poured love into her. It had happened. And she felt stronger for it. Equally suddenly, equally without warning, Jo had switched it off, had transformed himself back into the examining surgeon, with no thoughts or feelings except for what he was doing, a bronchoscopy on her father.

That was as it should be. He'd spared a brief moment to support her, and then gone straight back to the job. How had he known, though, how much she had needed that support at that precise moment?

Somehow he had known, and he had given it to her.

She had no idea how long their personal private communication had lasted. It had seemed like hours, but had presumably been no more than a few short moments. Not long enough, she hoped belatedly, for Don or anyone to have noticed.

She was out of luck here. Don had noticed, and remembered, too. Over a jar in the Lamb that evening he told his opposite number in the accident unit about it. 'It was extraordinary. There we were, in the middle of this bronchoscopy, and Standish was doing it himself—which was a bit of a disappointment to me, I can tell you—he'd let me do quite a bit on the previous one, after demonstrating on the first patient we had this morning, and there was I thinking maybe he was going to let me handle the final patient on my own. But no joy. Actually it turned out the patient was Sister Rutherford's father, so I suppose he felt he more or less had to do it himself. Anyway, there he was in the middle of it, and suddenly he asked Sister if she was all right, and she said she was—I hadn't spotted anything wrong with her, but Standish must have done, because he shot this question at her out of the blue. She told him, perfectly calmly, that she was all right, thank you, but their eyes, would you believe, stayed locked together. Oh, not for more than a few seconds, I don't suppose. But something happened between them, I'm certain of it. Is there anything on the go there, I wonder? Have you heard anything?'

'They were in here together, one evening last week.'

'Were they now? Must keep my eyes skinned. Anyway, soon after that, this bronchoscopy really took off. What a turn-up for the books.'

'Why, what happened?'

What had happened had been that as Jo examined Daniel's lungs, and reached the suspect area, his body stiffened, and he frowned.

Both Alix and Don picked it up. They knew he'd found something. Alix prayed silently. Hopelessly, she knew, but it was all that was left to do, and she did it. Please God, don't let it be malignant. Don't let it be. Please God.

To her astonishment, her prayers were answered.

Jo said, in a voice that emanated a quiet sort of triumph, 'Well, well, what have we here? Who'd have thought it? Daniel, I'm happy to tell you—'

He was *happy* to tell him? Alix could hardly believe her ears. What had he found?

'—you definitely haven't got lung cancer. You can forget all about that possibility. What you've got in this lung of yours is something far simpler that we can deal with quite easily.'

Daniel's eyes were fixed on Jo like lasers, and Alix's weren't much different. Suddenly the air of the little examination room was vibrating. Don had a broad grin and his eyes sparkled, though he didn't yet know what Jo had found, and the student nurses were bright-eyed and eager. This was one of those moments everyone in medicine treasured, when suddenly there was no place to be except in this hospital at this instant. These were the moments that made everything—the hard work, the thankless seniors, the grumpy juniors, the broken nights and interrupted meals—not only worthwhile, but a privilege.

'What we saw on that X-ray of yours was a ball of fungus. That's what's been causing all this misery. Not a growth at all. Just a fungal infection, indistinguishable in its X-ray appearance from a growth. You won't need surgery.'

Daniel was radiant, and Alix's eyes glowed as she listened.

'I can deal with this now, with the bronchoscope. I'll get it out immediately, and then you'll need a course of an antibiotic, and after that you'll be as good as new. You're a lucky man. There's nothing wrong with you that can't be cured, and within a month or two. I'll just ask Don to have a look at this, if you don't mind, and then we'll go ahead and remove it. Come along, Don, what do you make of this, eh?'

Don stared down the bronchoscope, and said nothing.

Jo took pity on him. 'A mycetoma, would you say?'

'If you hadn't said so, I wouldn't have had a clue.' Excitement made him incapable of any cover-up.

'Yes, that's what it is. You'll recognise it next time you come across it, though.'

'I certainly will.'

'Right, we'll get on with it. We'll do it now, Sister. Suck out this mycetoma, and then you can take Daniel home. All over, bar the antibiotic. How's that?'

'Terrific,' Alix said. She would have liked to sing and dance and jump about. Instead she reached for the suction apparatus.

CHAPTER TEN

A Dinner Party at Field End

DANIEL went to bed that afternoon and slept more soundly than he'd done for months. Alix went over to see him at about six o'clock and found him awake, a little husky, but unmistakably all stations go.

'A nuisance,' he said, 'that Celia can't get down here before Friday. I'd like to get straight back into the book.'

'It'll do you no harm to have a bit of a rest,' Alix said firmly, though she knew she'd be speaking to deaf ears.

Daniel snorted, and then winced. 'That hurt,' he said indignantly.

'Well, you're bound to be a bit sore for a day or two, as well as tired out. And then Jo's going to put you on this course of antibiotics. You ought at least to lie low for a few days—what you really need, of course, is a super holiday.'

They glared rebelliously at one another. Daniel wanted to snort again, but stopped himself in time, and said only, 'Getting back to the book will do me more good than any holiday.'

'I'm not so sure. What you need is to relax, lie around in the sun. Only there isn't any. You wouldn't like to take off for Miami, I suppose? Or Bermuda?' She knew it was hopeless, but she had to try.

He scowled. 'No way. Leave it alone, there's a good girl.'

Alix dropped it, but only for the time being. 'Have a quiet time for the rest of the day, anyway,' she suggested. 'Later on, I'll make you some scrambled eggs, or something like that, and then you can have an early night.'

'Did you say Jo was going to look in?' Daniel asked.

'That's what he said.'

'I'll open some champagne, then. We can have a celebration. Don't think I don't realise what I owe to you two, you *and* Jo. If I'd paid more attention to you I wouldn't have had to go through all this worry, or have felt so rotten for months. You were right and I was wrong.' He ruffled her hair affectionately, a habit of his when he was feeling fond of her, and one she'd treasured when she'd been younger, though she could have done without it now.

'Champagne would be super,' she said mildly, though inwardly she was almost ecstatic. This day that she had dreaded was going to end with champagne and Jo Standish. The time and the place and the loved one. For once everything was going to coincide. Best of all, Daniel was all right. He wasn't going to die. And Jo would be here at any moment to drink to the future in champagne.

'I'll put a bottle on ice,' was all she said.

The champagne on ice, Alix decided to go upstairs to change. Jeans and one of her oldest sweaters didn't seem the right gear for drinking champagne with Jo. But what was? Very likely he'd stay only for a glass, however many bottles Daniel might want to stash away for the celebration. Jo was a busy surgeon and might well have other patients to visit this evening. Or he might be needed in the accident unit. She could hardly don her best beaded and slit cocktail outfit for one glass of champagne with Jo in the early evening at Field End.

She went up the softly gleaming elm staircase and along the balcony to her room, and looked through her cupboards.

She'd play it cool. This was a cottage in the country. Right. She'd dress the part. She took out her plain but ludicrously expensive Burberry kilt, pulled on her beige cashmere sweater, fastened her pearls, and brushed her hair into a sleek and shining cap.

When she opened the door to Jo he was stunned. The sexy urchin with the spiky hair he adored, even though it had taken time for this reaction to become apparent to him. The impeccable Sister Rutherford, crisp and precise, he was only beginning to grow used to. Now the lady of the manor opened the door, and he'd never met her before.

He recognised the great grey eyes, though. And where this morning they'd been filled with anguish, this evening they were warm and welcoming. Even inviting, he suddenly grasped with a shock. From her dress you could not know her. Never in a thousand years. Tonight her dress informed the casual eye that she was correct and untouchable. But she wasn't. She was lovable.

To the enormous surprise of both of them, he took the soft warmth that was Alix Rutherford into his arms, hugged her, and kissed her on the cheek.

It had nearly been on the mouth, but somehow he hadn't quite made it. Not after this morning's bronchoscopy. Sister Rutherford was too near for that sort of clinch, which might far too easily get out of hand. Whatever he felt about her—and he wished he knew what it was—she was still his Sister-in-Charge, still his patient's daughter, and he remained the consultant visiting that morning's bronchoscopy.

Alix didn't work any of that out, of course. All she knew was that for a brief moment of timeless joy she was held where she longed to be. In Jo's grip, against his heart, with his cheek brushing hers. If only time would stop, and she could stay locked in his arms for ever.

She stepped back, he released her.

She said, 'Dad's expecting you. He's in a celebrating mood, and there'll be champagne. First of all, though, he wants me to take you through to his writing room.' Daniel had been specific about this, insisting on it, and Alix wondered if she ought to let Jo know what a break with tradition it was. No one, normally, was allowed to cross the threshold. It was some sort of measure of Daniel's gratitude to Jo, she suspected, that he'd arranged to meet him there, in the holy of holies. Jo couldn't know this. Ought she to tell him?

'I've never been up to the writing room,' Jo remarked as she led the way out through the kitchen and into the lobby.

'He doesn't usually allow anyone in. You're privileged.' There. It was said. He could make what he liked of it.

From the writing room, thundering down the stairs to meet them, came the opening bars of Brahms' Academic Festival Overture. The celebration had begun.

Jo heard the Brahms—no one could have failed to—but it hardly impinged on his awareness. All he took in was Alix's slight back, as she preceded him up the stairs, her wonderful legs and the soles of her highly polished brogues. All he felt was an overwhelming urge to put his arms round her and hold her for ever.

She led the way into the writing room, and Daniel rose from his desk to greet them.

'What a fantastic room, Daniel. I never realised you had anything like this up here,' Jo enthused.

'It's a nice room, isn't it?' Alix agreed equably,

though she wanted to jump about and shout. Jo was here, with her, in Daniel's writing room where he'd never been before, and suddenly everything had come together. Everything was right in her world. Soon there'd be champagne, to celebrate her father's victory over disease and death, and to celebrate Jo and herself pledging their troth.

Pull yourself together, Sister Rutherford. This is your chief, remember? Your father is his patient—and thank God for that—and you are his Sister-in-Charge. Nothing more. Snap out of this adolescent dream world. Wake up to reality.

Jo and Daniel were talking about the writing room.

'Yes, I had it and the garage built at the same time, and I designed it myself to suit myself,' Daniel was saying.

Jo was rambling about the big room with its tall bookcases, its great refectory table facing the window that looked over the fields to the sea, and Daniel's massive oak desk backing the bookcases and facing a wall of filing cabinets. 'I don't like a view when I work,' Daniel explained. 'The table is for sorting out papers, spreading my drafts around, doing research—I like to be able to look over the countryside then.'

'It's terrific. No wonder you spend a good deal of time here. I would. No one would be able to dig me out from here except for the most dire emergency.' So he said, but even as Jo spoke he knew perfectly well that if Alix was to be found in the other part of the house, nothing would have dragged him from her side.

'I'm fond of the room,' Daniel admitted. 'And of course I enjoy working. My bed's over there.' He jerked his head towards a low bay of bookcases that stretched out on the far side of his desk, and Jo saw for the first time that there was a low divan against the far wall, covered with a striped Swedish blanket.

'I'm pretty well self-contained,' Daniel continued. 'The bathroom's out there on the landing—you passed it as you came in. So I'm afraid I do tend to disappear for weeks on end when I'm flat out writing. I've a balcony too, for when I want to take the air.' He gestured towards the end wall, facing west, where double doors opened on to a wide balcony that appeared to jut out over the garden.

'The terrace where we sit in summer is underneath,' Alix commented.

Jo looked round the bookfilled room, with its antique oak and glowing Persian rugs that must, he suspected, have cost a fortune—or at any rate, several film options—and knew that Daniel had built himself not only a workplace but a retreat. This was his pad, where he belonged, and to hell with the rest of the world. This was where he had come when he had felt so ill and refused to admit it. Here he could forget the world and its dangers, be alone with his writing and, if death overtook him, he'd have died among his familiar friends. Fortunately, though, he hadn't died, and he wasn't going to die. What he was going to do was accept treatment, follow it, and get well. Alix would see he did.

She was sitting on the big leather couch that faced the open hearth, and Jo looked at her and suddenly found that he'd grown accustomed to all her disguises. She was Alix, the girl he loved. The girl he was going to marry. She was the same girl, whether she looked, as now, like an advertisement for the country life, like his crisply starched Sister-in-Charge, or like the hottest bit of property in Halchester. He loved her whether her hair stuck up in purple spikes, or lay flat and close to her head, dark and glossy and asking for his fingers to caress it.

She was his Alix.

Daniel was pouring champagne. He handed a tall fizzing glass to Jo, another to Alix.

'Your health,' Jo said, and raised his glass.

'Oh well, yes, I suppose so.' Daniel was embarrassed. 'But I didn't open the champagne to wish myself good health, exactly. It was to say thank you to you and Alix for all you've done. Between you, you've given me back my future, and I just wanted you to know that I appreciate it. Very much.' By now his voice was a mutter and could barely be heard against the Academic Festival, still roaring its head off.

Jo, watching Daniel's lips and concentrating, succeeded in hearing every word, and now he raised his glass again. 'To your future, then, Daniel. And to the success of the new book.'

This worked. Daniel, his embarrassing thank you speech safely off his chest, suddenly beamed, and said almost triumphantly, 'You know, I think it may be the biggest success I've ever had.'

The Brahms crashed to its own triumphant conclusion, and the tape switched itself off.

Into the quietness that followed, Daniel remarked, 'Alix was wanting me to have a holiday, but of course I must get on with the book as soon as I can.'

'You need a bit of a break, Dad,' Alix pointed out, without the least hope that Daniel would pay any attention.

'You've had a hard time, you know,' Jo said, also without much expectation of results. 'I've brought you some tablets to take, that should make short work of this mycetoma that's been making you feel so rotten. But for the next two or three weeks you still won't be up to much, health-wise. If you could take a break, have some fresh air and a bit of graduated exercise, you'd be much fitter—more able to do justice to the final draft of this very special book,' he added craftily.

To his astonishment—and even more to Alix's—
Daniel appeared to agree. 'I certainly shall need all
my energies for the next lap. Alix was talking about
Miami or Bermuda, but I don't want to fly for hours,
and I don't think I'd like hotel life in Miami very
much.'

'Somewhere nearer at hand, then,' Jo suggested.
'The Canaries, perhaps—Lanzarote?'

'That volcanic moon landscape—you either love it
or loathe it, and personally I loathe it.'

That disposed of Lanzarote.

But was Daniel actually proposing to have some
sort of holiday, Alix wondered? She had imagined he
would be impossible to shift.

What neither she nor Jo guessed was that Daniel
had had such a pasting, up here in his writing room,
trying to complete the draft of this book that mattered
so much to him against a background not only of ill-
health but of despair, that he had, for the first time
ever, turned against his writing room. This was what
the champagne was really for, this was why he had
decided to invite Jo in. He was trying to exorcise the
misery that still lay heavily around in what until
recently had been his favourite place, not only a
refuge but a launching pad.

'All the same,' he volunteered, 'I think you're both
right. I do need some sort of break. I thought I might
got to Switzerland.'

'Splendid idea.' Jo agreed at once. He knew when
to latch on to a good opportunity. Any sort of break
would be better for Daniel than staying here and
working non-stop, even Switzerland in November.

Switzerland, Alix was thinking. Of course. She'd
been slow. She ought to have remembered how
Daniel felt about Switzerland. It had always been his
home from home. He'd been at school there, and he
often returned.

'I could work in Switzerland,' he was saying. 'I can concentrate there. All I'd need to do is sort out what books I need to take with me, and I'd be ready to go—in any case, it's no distance. I could fly back to the London Library any day I needed to.'

'Of course,' Alix agreed faintly. Change his books by plane—why not?

'Celia could come out there to stay, too,' he added with immense satisfaction. 'She might enjoy a few days in Vevey. Be a nice change for her.' He thought about this briefly, and nodded to himself. 'I'd like to give her a bit of a treat—I'll give her a ring tomorrow, sound her out.' The prospect entranced him. 'You, too, Alix,' he added belatedly. 'Care for a weekend or two in Switzerland?'

'Love it.'

'More champagne?' Daniel began filling their glasses again, and the evening turned into the party he'd wanted it to be. 'I'll ring Mme Chardonnay in the morning, too,' he announced over his own full glass. 'Vevey, here I come.' He was expansive now, and the misery that had haunted his writing room had vanished, exactly as he had hoped it might, with champagne and company. The future beckoned him, where for weeks—months—it had been terrifying him. A plan he'd thought he'd have to abandon for ever came to life again and filled his horizon. 'Madame,' he remarked for Jo's benefit, 'owns an apartment house overlooking the lake at Vevey. I've often stayed there. Very comfortable. Alix knows it well.'

'That's right. Super place.'

The depression that Daniel had shed suddenly enveloped Jo like a blanket. No more Saturday chess with Daniel. He and Alix would be in Switzerland. He wouldn't see Alix from Thursday at five p.m. until the following Monday. Long weekends without Alix, that's what the future offered him. And he didn't care for it. However, he had to put a good face on it. A break in Switzerland was the right move for Daniel, and must be encouraged.

'When will you go?' he asked, sounding to both Alix and Daniel as if he personally were quite prepared to push Daniel off tomorrow morning, if not tonight.

'Ah, that's more difficult. I'll have to work that out. I'm not seeing Celia until Friday, and then I'll need to have a bit of time sorting out my ideas, and assembling the books I'll need to take, and so on. I can hire a typewriter out there, that's easy, I've done it before. Just pick up the telephone and order the same model as I use here, and someone comes round with it within an hour or two. The Swiss are good like that. So some time next week, I should think, provided Madame has a vacancy.'

'Not much doubt of that. She'll turn someone out if she has to, for you.' Laughter lurked in Alix's grey eyes now, Jo saw.

'Got a soft spot for Daniel, has she?'

'Soft as butter. He can do anything with her. Feather-bedded when you go there, aren't you, Dad?'

Daniel grinned in a lighthearted way Jo had never seen before. 'You could put it like that.' His eyes were dancing too, but this failed to affect Jo in the same way.

However, he pulled himself together and addressed himself sternly. He was making a professional call on a patient, not having a champagne party with a girl-friend. What he'd like to do would be to scoop Alix up and take her off to the best meal Long Barn could produce. What he had to do instead was to drink the last of his champagne, refuse a refill, and get out. Daniel needed a quiet evening and an early night, after some sort of light supper, to be provided, unfortunately, by Alix. No way could he gather her into his arms and take her out. She had to stay here and look after Daniel.

He carried out this programme to the letter, and inside three minutes was outside starting up his Volvo, having paused only to hand over the tablets for Daniel, accompanied by a quick word as to dosage.

Alix stood at the door and watched him go. The evening had started so marvellously, but now it was over. She shook her head, irritated with her own expectations, and set off to the kitchen to make scrambled egg for Daniel.

The rest of the week passed in a flash, but with hardly a sight of Jo. On Wednesday he spent the day in the accident unit, and the day centre had to make do with the thoracic registrar and the orthopaedic houseman, while on Thursday Jo was apparently in the main theatre working his way through a long list with the thoracic registrar, while the day centre had its own registrar, back from yesterday's stint in the accident unit, and the orthopaedic houseman again. But no Jo.

On Thursday evening Celia arrived from London in a very pretty heather mixture tweed with a smoky blue cashmere, her eyes sparkling with excitement and plans for Daniel's book. She and Daniel talked late into the night, and then spent Friday closeted in the writing room, even eating a sandwich supper there, after which Daniel drove her to the station for the last train. He returned, tired but clearly exhilarated, to inform Alix that Celia was not only happy with the book, but with the idea of flying out to Vevey for further discussions. 'So if I can just whip right through the draft again, checking on what we decided, and go up to the London Library early next week, then I might be able to take off for a couple of months. I rang Mme Chardonnay, and she's got an apartment for me, available from next weekend. Jo said he'd come for a game of chess tomorrow afternoon—' Well, it would be nice at least to catch sight of him, at any rate, thought Alix. '—so I can tell him then what I've arranged. I must say, I'll rather miss my weekly games of chess with him.'

'Get him to fly out to Switzerland too,' Alix suggested flippantly.

Daniel took her seriously. 'I doubt if he'd want to spare the time. Tell you what we might do, though— how about inviting him to stay on afterwards for dinner? We could get Woody to stay late and do us one of her best meals. Ages since we had a dinner party, and I'd like to demonstrate some gratitude to Jo, even if only to ask him to one of Woody's super spreads.'

'I've got someone from the Central coming down for the day tomorrow,' Alix said unwillingly. 'But he needn't stay on—he's only supposed to be coming for the day.'

'Can't very well pack him off back to London, if he's travelled down to see you especially. Who is he, anyway?'

'David Hurst. A registrar I used to know quite well. But—'

'Have him to dinner, too, then. Someone for Jo to talk to—he must be tired of hearing all about my book. He'll enjoy some news from the Central—so will you.'

'I suppose so,' Alix agreed unenthusiastically. What on earth had made her give in to David's pressure? He'd rung her on three or four occasions since she'd been at home, trying to persuade her either to come up to London for dinner and the theatre, or to ask him down to Field End. Each time she'd put him off, but for some reason she was now totally unable to comprehend, when he rang on Friday saying he had an unexpected free weekend, and how about if he came down to see her at last, she'd given in and asked him for the day on Saturday. It had been the 'at last' that had done it—she'd felt unkind, and told herself that she could hardly refuse to meet him ever again. After all, they'd been friends, they'd never actually quarrelled. Besides, it might do her good to see an old friend from the Central, take her mind off Jo and all her crazy dreams about him. David might not be her favourite person, but at least he was someone from the Central, and Daniel was quite right, it would be nice to hear all the news.

'So talk to Woody about food, would you? And I'll open some of the best claret.'

Woody was delighted at the prospect of a dinner party, and sacrificed her Saturday evening without a murmur. 'A long time since we had a proper dinner party here. It'll be nice to get out the best glasses for once, and the Royal Worcester. I always say it's a pity we don't use it more often, but your father's never been bothered about that sort of thing. And you ought to put on a bit of a celebration, now that we know your dad's going to be all right after all. That's a big relief, I must say. So now, what would you like to eat? You want something nice for this boy-friend of yours coming down from London especially, I expect.'

'Oh, he doesn't matter,' Alix said unguardedly.

'Doesn't matter? What do you mean? Why did you invite him?'

Why the hell had she? She wished she knew. 'Honestly, Woody, I don't know. I didn't really want him to come, but he was—well, he was fairly determined, and I couldn't quite see how to put him off, not without telling a lot of lies—and now I just wish he wasn't coming, that's all.'

'He's keener than you are, is he?'

Alix wriggled. 'In a way, I suppose.' But not in the

way Woody imagined. 'I don't think he's particularly keen on me, to be honest. He's just keen on Dad's Porsche.'

Woody laughed. 'One of those, is he? Like my Sam. Oh well, men are all the same, dearie. Children, the lot of them.'

Not Jo, Alix thought. She had enough sense, though, not to impart her thought to Woody, who returned to the more important problem of food.

'Venison? In red wine?—if your dad's thinking of opening some claret. How would that be, do you think?'

'Delicious.'

They planned the remainder of the meal, put the Royal Worcester china into the dishwasher for a whirl, followed by the Edinburgh crystal, and then Alix went out into the November garden to see if there was anything to fill the big vases. She was beginning to cheer up. Even if David was a dead weight, the dinner party would be fun.

The dinner party was no fun at all. More of a disaster.

Alix had already had lunch with David and her father, throughout which David had, she considered, almost fawned on Daniel. Too late, she remembered what one of her friends had said: 'Watch David with a pundit, crawling and buttering him up. The oozing and sucking up that goes on around anyone who might advance his career turns me right off. There's a side to David I don't go for—and neither will you.'

Filled with embarrassment, on quite whose behalf she wasn't sure, she took him off almost before he'd downed his coffee, and walked him along the cliffs in a howling gale, shouting question after question at him about her friends at the Central rather as if she were a quick fire examiner, until it was time to return to join Jo and her father for tea.

That was when the real trouble began. Jo took an instant dislike to David, and spent the remainder of the day cutting him down to size—a job, as Alix knew only too well, at which he excelled.

What she didn't know, never guessed, was that Jo was desolate. Exactly as he'd warned himself so many times, Alix was already committed to someone at the Central. Quite likely she had fixed this bloke's visit deliberately, as a gentle intimation to him that he was too late. Perhaps she had seen that he was getting too interested in her. So she was trying to remind him, before he became too involved with her, that she had someone in her life. Someone she cared about.

He'd been out of his senses to assume that he could just walk in and grab her. She was a loving daughter to Daniel, he'd soon found that out. Now he was discovering there was someone else she loved, at the Central.

He ought, he informed himself bitterly, to be glad, for her sake, that this David Hurst, rot him, had come rushing down to Halchester after her on his first free weekend.

He wasn't. He was devastated.

What's more, as the evening wore on, in spite of what should have been the benign influence of Daniel's memorable claret and Woody's superb cooking—angels on horseback, followed by the venison casserole so magnificently set off by the claret, and then the lightest and shortest of pastry enclosing blackcurrants from the garden—Jo became steadily more convinced that David Hurst was not half good enough for Alix Rutherford.

The big living-room at Field End was looking its best, the refectory table set with shining silver, the tall-stemmed glasses of Edinburgh crystal and Royal Worcester china, candles flickering in massive silver candlesticks over the centrepiece of St John's wort that Alix had picked that morning, still with a few lingering yellow flowers amid the vivid green and red berries. At the other end of the room the log fire blazed in the open brick fireplace, while a great vase of coppery beech leaves stood at the turn of the stairs and bowls of chrysanthemums scented the air. None of this, though, could hide from Jo the inescapable fact that his heart was breaking. At the same time he was ragingly furious with Alix for daring to prefer this handsome slob, David Hurst, over himself. If it was the last thing he could do for her, he would at least see to it, if he could, that she didn't blight her life for ever by throwing herself away on this cardboard nonentity. He set himself to demolish this cocky young registrar from the Central, disparaging or flatly contradicting anything he said. He snapped Alix's head off, too, though this was unintentional, a spin-off from his personal agony.

Daniel was no help whatever. He was in almost the same quandary as Jo. He loved Alix, and he found he didn't think David Hurst nearly good enough to marry his daughter. Jo had sense. He could see the chap was no good. Daniel, normally a quietly attentive host, tonight stepped out of line and did his best to second Jo's demolition job.

That left only Alix to look after her unfortunate guest. She had little inclination for the effort, but she blamed herself for having been so silly as to invite David in the first place, and duty drove her to protect him now he was here. He was outclassed, poor old David, and she owed it to him to see that he didn't have too bad an evening.

Miserably, she sat at the head of the table, glowing in the candlelight, a beautiful hostess with huge grey eyes, in a wonderful grey velvet dress and Zoe's amethyst pendant, looking her best, hating every second, watching three problem men sniping at one another.

She was thankful at last to be able to suggest they moved over to the fire for coffee, and escaped, she imagined, to the kitchen—Woody had long ago left, after dishing up the casserole.

It would have to be David who followed her out and offered his assistance. She wanted to bite his head off, and instead was guiltily honeyed. He carried the heavy silver tray with the Georgian coffee pot and the Royal Worcester cups and saucers through for her. Exactly like a devoted husband, Jo thought bleakly.

'Black,' he snapped, in answer to her enquiry. 'No, no cream. No sugar.' The words shot out like bullets. He wanted to exterminate David. He wanted to shake Alix until her teeth rattled. He wanted to creep away out of sight and cry for days, for this lovely girl whose life he'd dreamed he might share, whom he'd lost to this worthless oaf with his handsome grinning face and his stupid blond crinkly hair. He drank his coffee far too fast, scalding his tongue, crashed his cup and saucer back on to Alix's tray, and announced he had to be going.

Daniel saw him out, and then cravenly retreated through the garage and upstairs to his writing room.

This left Alix with David, and nearly an hour to go before his train. She clattered cups and saucers busily, stood up. 'I must take this through to the kitchen and clear the table.'

Not what David had had in mind. But by now, not unnaturally, he was more than a little unnerved, and he meekly pursued Alix with more dishes and glasses as she moved backwards and forwards between the dining-table and the kitchen. With his assistance, she filled the dishwasher, and then transferred the remains of the venison to a smaller casserole. After this she was able to glance at her watch, exclaim in false surprise that it was nearly time to leave for the station, and offer him the downstairs cloakroom while she escaped upstairs. In her bedroom, she angrily and perversely donned one of her oldest and most hideous coats, pulled faces at herself in the mirror, and brushed her hair furiously into belligerent peaks. She then descended to drive him to the station in the Porsche and thankfully waved him away to the last London train.

Irritated with herself, David, and the entire evening, she drove back to Field End, where, restless and on edge, she fiddled about in the living-room, tidying up, plumping up cushions, and finally trying out alternative positions for the flowers she'd arranged earlier so happily. What on earth had she been so happy about?

She'd been happy because Jo was coming to dinner. That he might have been equally happy, and was now torn between anger and despair, never occurred to her.

CHAPTER ELEVEN

Alix and Jo

BEFORE the next week was out, Daniel had moved to Vevey. As far as Alix could tell, he was in daily touch with Celia, holding long telephone coversations over each chapter.

His conversations with Alix were less frequent, but enormously cheerful—in fact he was still on the high that had set in immediately after his bronchoscopy. The apartment, he said, was magnificent, with a big balcony overlooking the lake, Mme Chardonnay's food was as good as ever, the service unobtrusive, and the rented typewriter worked perfectly. 'Jo was right, I needed a change.' Yes, he was taking the tablets, every mealtime. 'Wouldn't dream of forgetting, because they're working. I feel a different man, you can tell Jo.'

Tell Jo? She'd tell him if she saw him. But since that horrible dinner he'd hardly set foot in the day centre. It was his registrar, or the orthopaedic registrar, who taught the housemen, and when Jo did briefly appear he made it plain he hadn't a moment to spare, issuing staccato instructions to everyone, allowing no one to get a word in edgeways, and never pausing for coffee in her office.

Just when they'd been beginning to get along so well. It was that party that had changed everything. No getting away from it. It had been David. Jo hadn't liked seeing her with David.

But surely that could mean he was interested in her himself?

Nothing would have induced her to let David across the threshold if she'd known the effect it would have on Jo. But then she hadn't suspected Jo was even aware of her existence, other than as his Sister-in-Charge and Daniel's daughter.

There had been that evening he'd taken her in his arms, of course. But she decided that it had been no more than the friendly hug of an extroverted surgeon who knew what she'd been through.

Perhaps it had been more.

If so, by inviting David she'd thrown it all away.

What could she do now?

Nothing. She could hardly address him across the patient, the registrar and the house surgeon under tuition, informing him she wanted him to know he had the wrong idea about David Hurst. She didn't love him, and never had. There was only one human being she loved, apart from her father, and that was himself. Jo Standish.

Thank you very much. Are you ready for the next patient?

Nor could she throw these statements at him when he paused to deliver a few curt instructions at the entrance to her office. This week he'd formed the habit of holding on to the door handle while he hurled a couple of sentences at her across the room, presumably to underline the fact that he hadn't a second to spare.

Celia was coming to stay in Vevey for the weekend, Daniel was saying. She'd fly out on Friday and stay until Monday, and they'd work on the book. 'So I was wondering, how about if you came for the following weekend? How would that suit you?'

'Be great. I'd love to,' Alix told him. There was nothing for her in Halchester, that was for sure.

'Good. Thought you might be booked up with that David character.'

'*Him*? Oh, Dad, wasn't he *awful*? I was so ashamed of him. You know what it was, it was the Porsche. Once he'd set eyes on that, he was quite different.'

'H'm. That's a relief, anyway. Frankly, I didn't take to him much. Thought you must have fallen for his looks—handsome creep. Could hardly have been his intellect. Or his charm, as I said to Jo.'

'You—you *what*?'

'Said to Jo, dear—when I was seeing him out. I was a bit fed up, and I mentioned I wasn't much looking forward to taking him on as a son-in-law, and I couldn't imagine how you could be so deluded. Except that I do understand, unfortunately. What I did with your mother.'

'D—did you?' He'd never said so before. This telephone conversation seemed to be delivering nothing but a series of shocks down the line.

'Heavens, yes. A hopeless choice—two more ill-adjusted people—must have been out of my mind. Glad to know you've got more sense. But what on earth made you invite him down in the first place?'

'I wish I knew. He rang and invited himself, actually, and it seemed terribly unkind to put him off—what was more, he wouldn't jolly *be* put off, I'd have had to be really foul to shut him up. And then I thought anyway it would be nice to have news of everyone at the Central, you see, and also I suppose I felt I might have imagined how he'd suddenly changed when he saw the Porsche, and that I was misjudging him. How wrong I was.'

'Oh well, never mind. If there's nothing in it, it doesn't matter, does it? No need to get excited. What's an evening here or there? As long as I don't have to have him in the family I don't grudge him a square meal. I'd grudge him *you*, though. In fact, as

I said to Jo, I had half a mind to do my best to put a stop to it, except that it's against my principles to interfere.'

'Wh—what did Jo say?'

'Said to forget it, I had my book to think about. Quite right, too.'

'Yes, of course.' Naturally.

'Which is going very well, I'm glad to say.'

'Oh good. I am glad.' Alix tried to inject delight into her voice.

'So you'll come out the weekend after next, then, dear, that's agreed, is it?'

'Yes, that's fine, Dad.'

'I'll ring you nearer the day about your flight, and so on. Probably be a few things you could bring out with you.'

'Sure. Fine.'

Fine? Nothing was fine. Everything was awful. And it had all been her own doing.

It was a relief to escape from her own misery by shopping with Zoe in Halchester for most of Friday. Zoe was leaving on Tuesday for a business trip to Brazil with Humphrey. She always played fair with him. The theatre came first in the summer, his business commitments in the winter, and she loyally accompanied him even on the most boring journeys. 'Brazil, though, should be fun. And we're coming back through the States, with a break in San Francisco. I'm so sorry, though, darling, that this seems to leave you on your own here—trust Daniel to take off for Switzerland just when he's needed.'

'I shall be fine.' What a lie. But her dreams about Jo were not for sharing with Zoe—they'd be all round Halchester before supper. 'I'll be busy at the hospital anyway, and next weekend I'm flying out to see Dad.'

'I'm glad to hear it. Make sure he gives you a good

time, takes you out for a few meals. Don't let him shut himself away and write his book.'

Not surprising that Zoe and Daniel failed to get on. Zoe remained constantly under the impression that she had a duty (to whom, it was impossible to guess) to interrupt Daniel's writing and force him into leading a quite different existence. 'I shall be all right,' Alix said. 'I always enjoy Vevey, and he's got one of Mme Chardonnay's nice apartments.'

'Well, then, dear, if you're going to be enjoying yourself in Vevey next weekend, perhaps you wouldn't mind coming over tomorrow and on Sunday, and helping me. There's a mass of ironing to do still, as well as the actual packing. You're such a help, too, with lists. So clear-headed.'

So the weekend was surmounted with little opportunity to brood about Jo, other than for the last few minutes before she fell asleep each night—when she was so tired that sleep claimed her before she was able to plan a strategy. As a result, when Monday dawned, she was no nearer knowing how to approach Jo and inform him that his ideas about David were all wrong. That she had to do this she was certain. Somehow, no matter what it cost her, she had to make an opportunity to talk to him alone. She loved Jo, and he had been beginning to care for her—how seriously, she had no idea. But it was her own fault he'd felt rebuffed—if he had—and it was up to her to make him turn back—if it was possible. More than likely, she reminded herself miserably, he hadn't meant anything much by that hug and the friendly kiss on Tuesday evening. It had been no more than a friendly reassuring gesture. Because it lived on in her mind, so that she could feel still, as soon as she thought of that evening, the strength of his arms and the touch of his cheek so fleetingly against her own— none of this meant that it lived on for Jo. Very likely he'd forgotten it even before they climbed the stairs to the writing room, and what seemed the huge and almost unapproachable step of telling him about David was unnecessary. Silly. She was blowing a trivial episode up out of all proportion.

Somewhere in her depths, though, lived a girl who was entirely sure that none of this was any more trivial to Jo than it was to her. They cared about each other. Unfortunately, however, there were a lot of other more sophisticated voices within her, who kept on declaring that this was nonsense from start to finish. Jo Standish hardly knew she existed. He was her chief—and mainly absent, at that—and her father's friend.

The other girl, though, the one in love with Jo who went on insisting that he loved her back, was determined. She had to speak to him and tell him the truth about David. It had to be done, and soon, no matter how embarrassing, no matter how many people were hanging around with their ears flapping.

She could, of course, get Daniel to tell him. She could explain to her father, this weekend, how she felt, and persuade him to let Jo know that there was no question of David Hurst becoming his son-in-law.

No way was she going to hide behind her father. Hell, she and Jo worked together all week, every week. She wasn't so feeble, surely, that she couldn't make an opportunity to speak to him privately, no matter how grand and distant he chose to be.

Easier said than done, for grand and distant was what he turned out to be, this week even more than the week before. Not to mention monosyllabic, and whenever he came into the day centre he was surrounded by an entourage. Each morning he conducted a sort of high-powered teaching round, and then cleared off, striding away on his own, leaving them all in action. That he might be suffering never occurred to Alix.

Not a cup of coffee did he drink in her office. His registrar discussed the lists, and the only other contact she had with Jo was through his secretary, ringing across at intervals to say he was on his way, and he'd like this and that ready and waiting, or alternatively that he wasn't on his way, he was held up in the thoracic theatre, and to tell his registrar to go ahead, but rearrange the list, so that he'd be in time to do Mr So-and-so himself at the end.

However urgent Alix felt the need to talk to him to be, she could hardly interrupt him across the patient and the assembled housemen and students to explain about herself and David.

Monday passed, and nothing said. Tuesday, too. On Wednesday she was beginning to be desperate, but Jo didn't show his face in the day centre at all. There'd been a big pile-up on the motorway, she heard, he'd gone out with the ambulances and the cutting gear—the road had been closed for hours—and he'd spent the rest of the day and most of the evening in the accident theatre.

Now it was Thursday, and her last chance.

Alix took her courage in both hands. The first gap in the conversation she jumped in, saying with a firmness and authority she certainly didn't feel, 'Some time when you have a minute I'd like to have a word with you, sir.'

She never guessed the surge of hope these few phrases gave him. All he said was, 'Any time, Sister, any time.'

So now what did she say?

'When you have a minute to spare, sir. In my office, say?'

No one other than Jo took much notice, assuming she had a staff problem she needed to discuss. Jo, on the contrary, didn't think anything of the sort. He had a boy inside him who was in constant communication with the girl hidden away in Alix, and he was one hundred per cent certain that she was going to tell him something important. She was going to say she loved him, wanted him, adored him.

Nonsense. Pull yourself together, man. Snap out of it. 'I want to leave as soon as we've finished this case—Martin will take over then. Perhaps Staff could assist him, while you and I adjourn for a minute or two?'

'Certainly, sir.' Alix signalled to the staff nurse, who went to scrub up, wondering why on earth Sister's eyes had suddenly blazed so brilliantly across the little theatre.

Alix and Jo walked along the corridor towards her office, gowned, stripping off their gloves, their masks hanging.

'I'm flying out to see my father tomorrow.' Alix was abrupt. Only she knew she had chickened out at the last moment.

Jo's heart descended into his theatre boots. He might have known it. She was thinking only of Daniel. She wanted another prescription for him, that was what it was. 'You'll need another prescription,' he said crisply. 'I'll give you one.'

'Oh, thank you so much.' Alix heard herself gushing, and pulled herself together. Now or never. 'Actually, I hadn't remembered about the prescription. What I wanted to say was—was quite different.' She paused. Go on. Don't dither. You've got to say it, so come straight out with it. 'I wanted to tell you that— um—the other evening, I—I hated having—'

The telephone on her desk buzzed imperiously. Automatically she broke off and answered it, though later she asked herself why in the world she hadn't ignored it. 'Day surgery centre. Sister Rutherford.'

It was the transport office, checking the patients and their addresses for the homeward run. With one staff nurse taking her own place in the theatre, and the other supervising admissions as well as the recovery room, Alix couldn't dump the call on anyone else, and had to plod through the list with them, watching Jo write a note on her pad then walk out. She saw his broad back disappear with a feeling of helpless frustration. When the transport office eventually rang off, she put her hands over her eyes for a second or two. She could have wept.

No good sitting about feeling sorry for herself. She was supposed to be the Sister-in-Charge of this outfit, so she had better get on with running it.

She stood up, and then remembered Jo's note.

'Sorry, have to go,' he'd written. 'Will ring you at home p.m.' Underneath was a prescription for Daniel's antibiotic.

He'd ring her at home.

Her office was bathed in a rosy glow, everywhere sparkled—and herself with it. She walked back to the theatre treading on air, about sixteen feet tall.

At Field End, Woody had left her an enormous meal. Alix consumed it in a daze of anticipation and then sat by the fire with her coffee, dreamily waiting for the telephone to ring, occasionally vaguely planning what her exact words would be.

When the telephone rang she fell on it, glowing.

Daniel—with a long list of various books, notes, files and photocopies he'd like her to bring with her. 'Been making good progress this week, that's why I need all this. Oh, by the way, Celia's here for the weekend again—she came out last night. We want to get on.'

So it would undoubtedly be one of Daniel's writing weekends, not the sort Zoe had had in mind. She ought to have expected it—as usual, she'd be the unwanted third. Perhaps she needn't go—no, of course, she had to, to take all this stuff he wanted.

'Then I need some more shirts—and socks. Look them out and bring them, would you? And you might have a hunt for my grey cashmere pullover and bring that as well.'

She'd have to go across to the writing room to assemble all his papers and do the photocopying.

But she wouldn't be able to hear the telephone over there.

She waited another hour, did her own packing, and then decided she had to leave the telephone and collect Daniel's books and papers. If Jo tried to ring her, and she was over in the writing room, surely he'd try again?

Why should he bother? After all, he was only ringing because she'd told him she wanted to speak to him. She'd have to ring him herself. She could explain about being in the writing room, out of hearing of the telephone. That was it.

Long Barn told her that Mr Standish didn't answer and nor was his Volvo in the car-park. They rather thought he'd gone back to the hospital.

Of course the telephone finally rang when she was in the bath. She sent a tidal wave over the bathroom floor, raced, dripping, into her bedroom and grabbed the bedside telephone.

Jo, at last!

'Sorry to be so late, but I got called back to the accident unit. I'm just going into the theatre, so I'll have to be brief. What was it you wanted to talk about?'

Oh God. She couldn't mutter away about David and the dinner party when Jo was on the point of doing an emergency operation. Unforgivable.

She had to. Be brief, he'd said. And he'd meant it. But she must come out with it. No more hesitation. 'I just wanted to apologise,' she said clearly, 'for the other evening—the dinner when David Hurst was so awful. I didn't want to invite him, but he was worse than I thought he'd be, and I'm sorry you had to put up with him.'

'I didn't take to him, I must say.'

Jo's voice sounded strange. Presumably he must be wondering why on earth she'd made him ring her at this hour simply so that she could impart that bit of rubbish. 'That was all,' she said hastily. 'I just wanted you to know. Sorry to have interrupted you at a bad time.' She put the telephone down. There, it was done.

Dreamily she sat on the side of her bed visualising Jo scrubbing up and going into the accident theatre, until suddenly it struck her that she was wet, her duvet was sopping, and she had a full bath waiting.

CHAPTER TWELVE

Coming Home

EARLY the next morning Sam drove her to the airport. 'Hope you'll find your dad real better,' he said. 'Give him our best, me and the wife, won't you? Oh, and the wife said to be sure to tell you she'd have a nice meal waiting for you Sunday evening.'

'But Sam, she mustn't think of it. It's her day off.'

'Try stopping her, that's all. Said you wasn't coming back to an empty house and bread and cheese.'

Most people, Alix reminded herself fiercely, would consider her fortunate. The least she could do was to try and appreciate the care and cherishing lavished on her, instead of mooning about with a face like an old boot worrying about Jo Standish and what precisely he might be thinking of her.

It was when she reached Vevey that the real cherishing began—except that it was not directed towards her at all. Daniel and Celia greeted her together in the balconied living-room of Mme Chardonnay's apartment overlooking the lake. They were hand in hand, their eyes shining with delight in one another, and once again champagne stood at the ready.

Daniel and Celia were getting married. As soon—wait for it—as the book was finished.

'Oh—I see. How super. Gosh, I'm terribly glad.'
Why on earth hadn't she seen this coming? Had she
been blind? They were made for each other. 'Er—
why wait for the book to be finished? Why not just
get married?'

'No, we'll get the book completed first.' The
happy pair spoke in unison, but Alix thought she
caught a fleeting glimpse of longing in Celia's eyes.
It vanished so fast, though, that she couldn't be
sure she hadn't imagined it.

'Anyway,' she said, 'whenever it's to be, it's
marvellous, I'm so terribly glad. It'll be great, both
of you living at Field End, and—'

'Celia's keeping her job on,' Daniel interposed.
'And her flat in London. She'll fly out here to work
with me, just as she has been doing, of course. And
I dare say I'll pop back to the London Library and
spend a day or two at her flat. And when I go back
to Field End, we'll do the same. Can't afford to
lose her as an editor, I can tell you that.' He gave
his newly affianced bride a glinting, humorous look
that made him seem a boy again, a boy Alix never
remembered having glimpsed before.

'I may go part-time,' Celia said equably. 'After a
while, when the Press have grown used to the idea.
I'll probably be able to work mainly from home,
except when I'm actually with an author. That
should be quite easy to fix. Daniel will need a good
deal of time on his own, without me, when he's
writing.'

She was right, of course. Their plans seemed to
be made for them, offering a way of life almost
bound to succeed, Alix realised, and suddenly she
was immensely happy for them both. 'Terrific,' she
said, hugging Celia and then Daniel. 'So what about
this champagne? Let's drink to your future.'

Daniel looked relieved, and Alix saw that he

must have been uneasy about her reaction to his news. 'Champagne coming up fast,' he told her, grinning like a schoolboy as he began to fiddle with the cork. There was a satisfactory pop, and he filled the tall glasses.

They toasted each other, they drank to the future, Daniel drank to Alix and to his restored health. 'At one stage I didn't think I was ever going to be a good enough life to ask her to marry me,' he told Alix.

'You look loads better already—better than you've done for months,' she said. He'd lost that grey pallor and the air of strain, and even seemed to have put on a bit of weight. 'You owe that to Jo,' she added, her eyes soft with longing.

Daniel leapt on her comment. 'That's right. We'll drink to Jo, shall we?' He raised his glass.

'To Jo,' they chorused, and for a brief moment Alix almost felt he was there in the room. Her spirits soared.

Hastily she forced her thoughts away from Jo and back to the engaged pair. They were, in fact, worth looking at. Daniel not only looked much fitter but seemed to have shed about twenty years, and his expression, whenever he glanced towards Celia, was open, unguarded, tender.

And Celia was blindingly happy. Of that there could be no doubt. Her face was alight with love, and she was prettier than ever in a soft smoky blue suede outfit that matched her eyes, while as she raised her glass to her lips Alix saw she was wearing a wonderful glowing sapphire.

'You look marvellous. That suede's a fantastic colour—perfect for you.'

'Except for my sweater, which is my own, it's a present from Daniel—from the suede and leather boutique here in Vevey. Daniel insisted on buying

it this morning—we took an hour or two off from
the book—'

'To buy clothes?' Alix asked faintly.

'Special occasion.' Daniel was short. 'We're going
to make up for it this afternoon, of course.'

She might have known it.

'We thought we'd persuade you to spend the
afternoon in the boutique,' Celia said. 'You're to
choose yourself an outfit too—it's all paid for, all
you need do is choose your colour, and get kitted
out.'

'Truly? Dad, I—' Alix began, overwhelmed.

'Celia's suggestion. So we'll have a bite of lunch
here—they should be sending it up any minute—
and then you can go shopping, and we'll get back
to the book. We'll all go out for a proper celebration
this evening.'

'You'll find there's a waistcoat and skirt, the
same as I'm wearing now,' Celia explained, 'and
then trousers, and various sorts of jacket. You're
meant to have the lot.'

'Wow! I can see I'm going to have a splendid
afternoon.'

In the boutique, Alix fell for black leather. It had
done incredible things for her once—so why not
again?

That evening she brushed her hair into wild peaks
and stared into her mirror dreaming of Jo for far
too long. Abruptly she straightened her shoulders,
told herself to stop being so idiotic, donned a black
silk shirt, black leather trousers and jacket, fastened
Daniel's diamond pendant at her throat, and strode
arrogantly behind Celia and Daniel through the
restaurant, where, the previous Saturday, Daniel
told her, he had proposed.

Not unnaturally, tonight they were engrossed in
one another, and in spite of her enjoyment of

superb cooking, Alix felt very much the unwanted third. Acute loneliness swept through her, and there in the crowded glittering restaurant, packed with the fashionable élite of Vevey, she longed to be back in St Mark's with Jo.

Annoyed with herself, she speared perfectly prepared scampi and tried to will herself into proper enjoyment. But none came.

Belatedly, Daniel apparently noticed she was with them. 'What shall you do tomorrow?' he enquired, spooning up a delicious confection of whipped cream and fresh fruit nestling in meringue. 'I'm afraid Celia and I will have to work most of the day.'

Suppressing an impulse to burst into tears and inform him, through sniffs, that she'd fly straight home after the meal and plant herself on Jo at Long Barn, Alix shook her head and said briefly, 'Not sure. Go for a walk, probably. By the lake.'

'Do that.' Celia focused on her. 'And then eat a huge lunch, why not? And sleep it off on the balcony in the sun. You look worn out. Afterwards we can have a nice tea together—Daniel will break for that, won't you, darling?' She directed an unmistakable 'you'd better, or else' glance at Daniel, who said he should be able to stop by tea time, he supposed.

So Celia was not going to be merely the junior partner, handmaiden and editor in this new marriage, Alix thought. Good for her.

Their coffee arrived. Celia poured. Daniel, to Alix's astonishment, failed to reach at once for his cigars. Instead, frowning, he took a peppermint provided by the management and munched morosely.

Alix goggled.

'Your father's given up smoking,' Celia told her. 'He decided the time had come.'

You mean *you* decided, Alix thought, though all she said was, 'I'm so glad. I'm sure it's wise.'

'Jo'll be amazed,' Daniel commented.

'I'll tell him,' Alix promised. And as she spoke those magic words, her loneliness vanished as if it had never been and suddenly she was glad to be with Daniel and Celia who had found each other, but even more delighted to be leaving them the next day to return to Jo and St Mark's and her job.

As she was swept smoothly towards Geneva and her flight home in the limousine summoned for her by Mme Chardonnay's minions, she reminded herself that now Daniel was not only fit and well but had Celia to look after him for the rest of his days, she could perfectly well go back to the Central and all her friends there.

Well, she didn't want to. Not any more. The Central had slipped away into the past. The future lay in St Mark's. Yearning after Jo might get her nowhere, but working alongside him was another matter. She wasn't giving that up. Whatever their personal relationship—and with luck it would be a good deal better this week than it had been last—she and Jo together *were* the day surgery centre. Her job there meant as much to her—no, more—than any other post she'd held.

Swissair decanted her punctually at Gatwick, and she scanned the crowd for Sam. She couldn't spot him. Amazing. Sam was never late. Always reliable.

Her gaze swept over the throng again. There, head and shoulders above the level where she'd been searching for Sam, stood Jo.

Their eyes met. He raised a hand, shouldered his way towards her.

She couldn't understand it. What was Jo doing

here? Who was he meeting? And where on earth was Sam?

'Hullo, good to see you.' His lips brushed her cheek in that coolly affectionate way he'd done before. Once. Now it was twice, and her knees shook, a warm glow spread through her and her spine tingled. 'Hullo,' she said weakly. 'What are *you* doing here?'

'Meeting you.' He was laughing at her. What could be going on? What was happening to her? To them both? 'Give me that.' He took her case, and made for the car-park. On the way he remarked casually, as if it explained everything, 'I rang Sam and told him I'd meet you.'

'Oh, I see.' But she saw nothing. Nothing except a galaxy of stars whirling round inside her head as she exploded into brilliant uncontrollable joy. But she had to control it. She must remain calm and self-possessed. Collected. Responsible. She was Sister Alix Rutherford, being met at the airport by her chief, the director of the day surgery centre at St Mark's. A kindly gesture on his part, but no more. She mustn't allow herself to read too much into it. She must pull herself together. 'You rang Sam?'

'That's right.' He was unlocking the Volvo, and appeared to be paying very little attention to her, Alix thought—though here, of course, she was in error.

He came round the car and settled her into the passenger seat, handing her the safety-belt as if she had been someone's great-grandmother who travelled by car with great ceremony perhaps once or twice a year. Little did she guess that he would have liked to have lifted her feet in for her. Even to breathe the same air was intoxicating. To touch the ends of her fingers as he passed her the seat-belt was electrifying. She was his Alix, and she had come home to him. He was going to keep her for ever. 'So it's the black leather get-up again, is it?' he commented, his eyes glinting. 'You look terrific.' His fingers slipped across her sleeve with the briefest of caresses.

Alix, considerably to her surprise, instead of throwing herself passionately into his arms and staying there succeeded in remaining calmly in her seat and fastening her belt. 'Yes,' she agreed. She had been afraid her voice might let her down, quiver and collapse into broken cries of abandoned love, but she was relieved to hear it coming out normally, as unruffled as if she'd been on a ward round.

To Jo she sounded detached and absolutely unreachable. After their short conversation on the telephone before he went into the theatre on Thursday night, he had spent a delirious weekend planning their future. She wasn't in love with that oaf David Hurst after all. What was more, she'd wanted him, Jo Standish, to know this, to be clear about it. And that could mean only one thing, he'd reminded himself at five minute intervals throughout the weekend. She cared about him.

But now here she was, beside him, cool and distant as ever, obviously totally in control of herself and her own life. Capable and independent. He must have been mad to suppose there was anything between them. For him she was the only girl in the world, now and for ever. But for her? She was his Sister-in-Charge. He was part of her working life, no more. Plainly she couldn't understand what had possessed him to drive here on Sunday evening to meet her when she'd been expecting Sam.

What on earth had made him imagine she'd be

staying in Halchester, to begin with, with him or anyone else? She'd taken the post at St Mark's only because her father was ill, she'd said so, and now he was better. St Mark's would lose her just as soon as she could work out her notice, and either she'd join Daniel in Switzerland or she'd clear straight off back to the Central. He'd been living in a lunatic's paradise all weekend.

He'd even, God help him, gone so far as to look at houses. He'd searched for a house for himself and Alix to live in, while they worked together at St Mark's.

After he'd put the telephone down on Thursday night, he'd been surging with superfluous energy. He wanted to take the next plane and chase after Alix to Geneva and on to Vevey. However, as he unfortunately happened to be on call for the accident unit throughout the weekend, he'd filled the long hours by thinking about her. His Alix, walking round the day centre in Sister's blue with her crisp white cap perched precariously, or muffled up in her theatre gown, her eyes large above her mask. Other pictures of her crowded in—Alix with her hair in purple spikes; Alix tired and wan in faded old jeans. Alix, his beloved.

Enthusiastically, he'd contacted the local estate agents and rushed round Halchester viewing the properties on their lists.

What was more, he'd found somewhere. He'd planned to take Alix to see it as soon as they'd consumed this meal Woody had insisted on preparing. He had the keys in his pocket.

A tiny Georgian gem, tucked away in a quiet alley below the cathedral, it was enchanting. The narrow road was cobbled still, the terrace of soft pink brick set back behind long front gardens.

Inside, at the end of a narrow hall, a staircase curved gracefully.

It had all been a lovely dream, nothing more. Here he was, awake and sane again, with Alix beside him, sexy as they come in black leather with her hair in ravishing spikes, but self-contained and unreachable, wrapped up in her own concerns, unaware—and uncaring—of his longing to hold her and love her. His entire plan had been nonsense. He set his lips and switched himself firmly back into a senior consultant talking to his highly competent Sister-in-Charge. 'Did you have a good weekend?' His voice was distant, polite. 'How was Daniel?'

To his amazement, she giggled. No other word for it. 'Terrific,' she assured him, and she was bubbling with laughter still. Not detached at all, as he'd thought, but bubbling over with a delight she wanted to share with him. 'He's stopped smoking— I was to tell you that, he said, but it's the least of it. He's got himself engaged to Celia. It's Celia who stopped him smoking, of course. Nothing to do with anything you or I have been saying—we could have saved our breath. They're going to get married—wait for it—as soon as the book's finished.'

Jo was bemused, though more by the unexpected change in Alix than by the news, which he'd hardly taken in. 'Um—who would Celia be?' he enquired doubtfully.

'His editor.'

'Oh, I see. Well, what do you know? Bully for Daniel.'

'So that's him off my hands,' Alix said with a brusque return to her Sister-in-Charge manner.

'Quite so.' Jo was the consultant. 'You'll be able to think about getting a post at the Central again. Moving back to London.' Goodbye, my darling, my beautiful love.

'Oh, I shan't do that,' she said at once. 'Heavens, no. I wouldn't dream of leaving St Mark's.' She gazed at him, wide-eyed with astonishment.

'You wouldn't?' You wouldn't? You wouldn't? The words thundered in his head.

'Oh no. The day surgery centre is where I belong now. I'm far too much involved in it to think of clearing off back to the Central at this stage. After all, you know, I've never been in at the opening of a new unit before, let alone been in charge of it.'

Once again, Jo began to reorganise all his ideas. Perhaps his dream hadn't been quite so imbecile. Perhaps, even, the keys to that house might still come in useful.

'I have to stay and see it firmly established.' Alix told him. 'It's my baby. It belongs to me and I belong to it.'

Jo saw his chance and took it. 'And to me,' he said firmly. 'Don't forget, you belong to me, too. All right?' He took her hand in his and held it securely.

'Very much all right.' Alix could hardly believe her ears, but she managed to get these four words out.

'Good. That's understood, then.' Jo gave her her hand back, patted her knee reassuringly, and moved out into the fast lane. He accelerated, passing everything on the motorway. He couldn't wait to get back to Field End. They'd have this blasted meal of Woody's, and then he'd take Alix to see the house and ask her to marry him. Next week, say. Why not?

Field End greeted them with a smell of roasting beef, furniture polish and chrysanthemums. Woody had washed all the paintwork, polished everywhere, and stripped Sam's greenhouse of half its stock. 'I wanted to liven the place up for you to come home to,' she explained, bringing in topside surrounded by roast potatoes. 'Now, who's going to carve this joint?'

'Shall I?' Jo enquired.

'Please,' Alix said, almost expiring from joy. She longed to add, 'please carve all my roasts for the rest of my days,' but bit the words back. All right, so she was right round the twist, but no need to advertise the fact!

Woody was surveying the loaded table—loaded, Alix vaguely noticed, with the Royal Worcester again, and the Edinburgh crystal. Woody had obviously decided this was an occasion. 'That's it. Everything seems to be there. So I'll be off now, Alix. You'll find a blackberry and apple pie in the oven, and the cheeseboard's ready on top of the fridge.'

'Thank you, Woody, that's super. Thanks terribly for coming in specially—it's great to come home to all this.'

At last she had gone, and they were alone.

Jo raised his glass. 'Here's to us.'

It was a commitment, and Alix recognised it as such. 'To us,' she echoed.

Their eyes locked.

'I found a house,' Jo said baldly. 'I thought we might go and look at it tonight.'

Alix went very still, but her grey eyes glowed with a light that told him all he needed to know.

'I hope you'll like it. I do. But if you don't, we'll just look for somewhere else.' He put down his knife and fork, and touched one of her fingers across the table. Then he picked up his knife and fork again and cut up his beef angrily. 'It's no good,' he told her accusingly. 'I simply dare not touch you.'

Alix cut up her own beef and wondered why they

had to eat the meal at all. 'Why don't we forget about this wretched meal? And—and just hold on to each other?'

Two chairs crashed to the ground, two pairs of knives and forks clattered on to Royal Worcester plates, and then at last they were holding one another as if they'd forgotten how to let go.

Two bodies melted into one, while the world shifted and changed for ever.

EPILOGUE

It was lunch time on Monday when Alix and Jo finally made their way along the cobbled alley below the cathedral to the Georgian terrace of soft pink brick, walked up the long paved path, stood under the small pillared portico while Jo unlocked the front door—a heavy panelled door with an arc of leaded fanlight above it—and stepped into the hall.

Alix's eyes followed the graceful turn of the stairs, and dwelt with utter content on the arched window on the half landing. 'Perfect,' she said. 'Though we'll have to get rid of this carpet. It's a disaster. How anyone could have chosen it for a house like this . . .' She shook her head. The previous owners had covered the floors with a garish swirl of orange and red on a hot pink background.

Jo's mouth twitched and he raised dark brows in apparent dubiety, though his eyes were alive with joy. 'You mean you think we should buy the place?'

'How could we possibly do anything else?'

'Come and see the living-room.'

It ran the full length of the narrow house, and had its original marble fireplace with a basket grate. 'This room must get the sun all day,' Jo pointed out, producing a compass from his pocket and gesturing to each window in turn. 'The window with the cathedral view looks east, and the front windows face west—we should get some glorious sunsets.' He glanced up at Alix for approval, and at once forgot about the cathedral and the sunsets. Here

181

she was, his Alix, in this house he had discovered for her. They were going to make their home here. He wanted to grab her and make wild glorious love to her in celebration; he wanted to throw her down this second on to the hideous carpet and show her the joy they were going to have together for the rest of their days. And then his mood changed, and he wanted only to hold her close, very quietly and gently, for hours on end, saying nothing, simply feeling her closeness and knowing she was his at last, and they were going to have a lifetime together. He kissed her forehead, her eyes, touched her cheeks with tender loving fingertips, and only then kissed her lips. 'My darling love,' he said. 'We'll get married, live here for years and years, and raise a huge family, shall we?'

'Yes, please.' She hugged him tightly.

'Come on,' he said reluctantly. 'We've less than an hour and we have to go over this house we've decided to buy.'

'My mind's made up. Doesn't matter if it's inconvenient, has dry rot in the basement and woodworm in the roof. We're having it.'

'In fact it's supposed to be structurally sound,' Jo told her. 'Or so the agent swore. Not that we won't have it very carefully surveyed. In the meantime, come on, let's go over it.'

Downstairs, in the semi-basement, there was a kitchen and a dining-room, a cloakroom too, and a door into a small paved and walled garden, again with the cathedral view. Upstairs, on two floors, there were five bedrooms and two bathrooms.

'It's a good deal bigger than I realised,' Alix commented. She grinned cheerfully. 'Quite big enough to raise this family you were mentioning.'

They kissed again for what seemed a brief moment only, or a long lifetime, neither of them could have said which, and then their lunch hour was over. They had to return to the hospital—Jo had outpatients, and Alix had the vascular surgeon tying varicose veins.

'I'll ring the agent,' Jo said as he locked the front door behind them. 'And the solicitor. I'll try and get hold of a good surveyor, too.' He paused. 'How about being married and in by Christmas? Think we could make it?'

'Why not?' Alix agreed, smiling brilliantly. Today anything was possible.

Somehow—mainly by a good deal of telephonic bullying—they did make it. Agent, solicitor, surveyor, decorators, department stores—none of them had known anything like it before.

The hospital had never known anything like it, either. Alix and Jo were the talk of thoracic surgery, the accident unit and the day surgery centre.

'Have you noticed,' they asked one another in the accident unit, 'how they can't bear to be apart? Their eyes are always searching for each other.'

'I think they're sweet.' A staff nurse sighed ecstatically, to the shock of two second-year students, who had supposed her to be hard-boiled.

The staff nurse from day surgery made her contribution. 'At first I thought she was just in another of her usual check, check and check again moods, but then I fell in. She was looking out for our Mr Standish, just in case he might have popped in without her spotting him. Her concentration's gone to glory—but aren't they lovely together?'

Everyone agreed that they were lovely together.

Over coffee in the common room, Jo's registrar embarked on his tale. These days his chief's eyes were always searching along corridors and round corners. 'When we discuss a case, he stares straight over my shoulder—I keep imagining he's noticed someone he wants to talk to, but it isn't that at all. He's watching out for a glimpse of his beloved. And when Alix actually does surface, you should see his face light up—talk about the happy couple.'

'Not wasting any time hanging about, either, are they?' the orthopaedic registrar asked. 'Married before Christmas, or so they say in the accident unit. Presumably it'll be a register office affair, at such short notice.'

'Don't you believe it. It's to be a cathedral wedding. The invitations are going out before the end of the week, Jo told me himself.'

'How on earth has he managed to book the cathedral for a wedding in Christmas week at no notice at all?' The orthopod was shaken.

'That's our Jo for you—and don't forget, six months ago he did have the Dean as a patient.'

'Of course—that explains it. Patients can be amazingly useful from time to time, can't they?'

'The florist was a patient too, so the flowers ought to be quite something.'

'I suppose the reception'll be at Long Barn? Do you think any of the rabble—you and me and a few housemen, I mean—might rate invitations?'

'Jo seems to be expecting half the hospital—half the Central, too, off the London train, including Leo Rosenstein and his wife. I've been told to look out for them and put them up front. I'm to be an usher, and so's Don—you could try offering, if you want to. He'd probably be pleased if you did.'

'OK. Will do.'

'You're wrong about the reception, though. It's to be in that house they're buying near the cathedral.'

'Good grief—I wouldn't have thought they'd have had time to complete the purchase, let alone furnish it and hold a wedding reception in it.'

The thoracic registrar laughed hollowly. 'If you'd worked for Jo you'd not have the slightest problem in believing any of it, I assure you. You layabouts in orthopaedics don't know what hustle means.'

Hustle was the name of the game, and somehow the house was theirs and ready for guests on their wedding day. 'After all,' Alix explained to a worried Woody, 'an empty house is fine for a party.'

Woody protested. 'That's all very well, Alix, but what about—'

'Mrs Armitage from Long Barn is doing the food and drink, and seeing to the clearing up afterwards, the Chapter House Florist is filling the place with flowers, and Jo and I are simply going to camp there for our honeymoon, and furnish as we go along. Though I've had the house recarpeted already—luckily we had a patient who's a carpet layer, and he managed to get acres of plain gold Wilton from the warehouse at wholesale rates. It's all down. Looks terrific. I've ordered plain holland blinds for every room, so we needn't bother about curtains to begin with, and they've measured up and are going to fit them tomorrow.'

'What about your dress, then?' Woody was not able to share in the general air of undiluted bliss. On the contrary, she was in a perpetual state of acute anxiety, convinced that with Daniel out of reach in Vevey and Zoe still in South America, something essential would be overlooked, and it would all be her fault.

'Oh, that's all fixed.' Alix was airy. 'Didn't I tell you?'

'No dear, you did not.'

'Zoe rang up, and I'm to have her wedding dress. She told me where to find it, and I've tried it on and everything. Dior. Fantastic!'

And so, three days before Christmas, hordes

poured down from the Central to Halchester Cathedral, for the wedding of Jo Standish, MS, FRCS, to Alix Rutherford, RGN. More hordes poured into the cathedral from St Mark's, Swissair decanted Daniel and Celia at the airport, Sam duly met them and drove them to Field End, where Alix, with Woody's assistance, was already radiant in Zoe's Dior gown.

Sam drove Celia and Woody to the cathedral, and returned for Daniel and Alix. He was, as ever, punctuality itself, and absolutely on time Alix paced up the aisle on Daniel's arm.

The organ thundered, Jo stepped forward, and the wedding service proceeded. Alix, everyone murmured, looked wonderful, a dream bride—and didn't someone say that drift of cream silk was *Dior*?

Jo, though, saw only her great grey eyes, fixed on his and brimming with love. He took her hand, they made their vows, he put the ring on her finger. They walked back down the aisle while the organ thundered again, and their guests turned and murmured and smiled. They smiled back, but none of it registered with either of them. They were together, and they were going to remain together for all the days there were.

Sam was not awaiting them at the entrance. They walked down the cobbled ways to their new home, followed by Daniel and Celia and their guests.

'Wot would you 'ave done if it 'ad bin pouring cats and dogs?' Leo Rosenstein wanted to know, his eyes glinting.

'We had contingency plans.' Jo was casual. 'Involving a fleet of cars, and a complicated drive round the one-way system. Fortunately it didn't come to it.'

'And y'r wife had her own contingency plan—I like y'coat, duckie. Smashing.'

Alix was wearing a full length duvet coat, padded and rippling in silk the colour of clotted cream. It had been a personal present to her from Celia, who had been much concerned about the walk from the cathedral to the house. 'I searched and searched in Vevey, and then Lausanne and Geneva,' she said. 'I was almost giving up hope. And then back in London I tracked this down in Pindisports in Holborn one lunch hour.'

The house welcomed them with sunlight and flowers everywhere, together with trestle tables groaning with food and drink. Champagne corks popped, everyone toasted bride and groom, Leo kissed Alix and drank her health. 'Here's to the best Theatre Sister I never had.'

But at last they were alone, in their own home, Daniel and Celia were unable, they had explained apologetically, to take any more time off from the book. They would not, either, they were afraid, be able to join them for a family Christmas at Field End. They were so sorry. They kissed Alix enthusiastically, shook hands somewhat formally with Jo, and climbed into the car to be driven by Sam back to the airport.

'Thank the lord for that,' Jo said unkindly. 'We can have Christmas here on our own.'

On Christmas Eve the weather turned cold and frosty. Alix put on her creamy duvet coat and they went to the midnight service at the cathedral, and afterwards walked home again down the cobbled alleys, to their long living-room, where a log fire scented the air and the floodlit cathedral was framed in the window.

'Happy Christmas, darling,' Jo said, and took her into his arms. 'The first of many.'

Happy Mother's Day

This Mother's Day, instead of the usual breakfast in be
why not ask your family to treat you to the Mills & Boon
Mother's Day pack. Four captivating romances to enthral yo

THE EMERALD SEA by Emily Spenser

A marine biologist finds herself out of her depth on an
Italian film set — and with the director.

THE MARRIAGE BED by Catherine George

A holiday in the Algarve becomes a nightmare when th
heroine is kidnapped in revenge for an injustice she knows
nothing about.

AN IDEAL MATCH by Sandra Field

Despite two broken engagements, a young woman still
believes in marriage — she comes to love a widower left with
three children but finds he had lost his faith in love.

ROUGH DIAMOND by Kate Walker

Can a successful businesswoman and a garage mechan
really bridge the gap between two such different backgroun

FOUR UNIQUE LOVE
STORIES IN A SPECIAL
MOTHER'S DAY PACK
AVAILABLE FROM
FEBRUARY 1987.

PRICE £4.80.

Bewitched in her dreams she awoke to discover the face of reality

The same dark hair, the same mocking eyes.
The Regency rake in the portrait, the seducer of Jenna's dreams had a living double.

But James Allingham was no dream, he was a direct descendant of the black sheep of the Deveril family.

They would fight for the possession of the ancestral home. They would fight against desire to be together.

Unravel the mysteries in
STRONGER THAN YEARNING,
a new longer romance from
Penny Jordan.

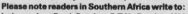